HONEY MOON

DOG DAZE

by
Sofi Benitez

with Joyce Magnin

Illustrations by Becky Minor
Based on the artwork of Christina Weidman

Created by Mark Andrew Poe

rabbit publishers

Dog Daze (Honey Moon)
By Sofi Benitez
with Joyce Magnin
Created by Mark Andrew Poe

Rabbit Publishers
1624 W. Northwest Highway
Arlington Heights, IL 60004

Illustrations by Becky Minor
Based on the artwork of Christina Weidman
Cover design by Megan Black
Interior Design by Lewis Design & Marketing

ISBN: 978-1-943785-19-3

10 9 8 7 6 5 4 3 2 1

1. Fiction - Action and Adventure 2. Children's Fiction
First Edition
Printed in U.S.A.

I can be brave.

— Honey Moon

TABLE OF CONTENTS

PREFACE

Halloween visited the little town of Sleepy Hollow and never left.

Many moons ago, a sly and evil mayor found the powers of darkness helpful in building Sleepy Hollow into "Spooky Town," one of the country's most celebrated attractions. Now, years later, the indomitable Honey Moon understands she must live in the town, but she doesn't have to like it, and she is doing everything she can to make sure that goodness and light are more important than evil and darkness.

Welcome to *Honey Moon*. Halloween may have found a home in Sleepy Hollow, but Honey and her friends are going to make sure it doesn't catch them in its Spooky Town web.

FAMILY

Honey Moon

Honey is ten years old. She is in the fifth grade at Sleepy Hollow Elementary School. She loves to read, and she loves to spend time with her friends. Honey is sassy and spirited and doesn't have any trouble speaking her mind—even if it gets her grounded once in a while. Honey has a strong sensor when it comes to knowing right from wrong and good from evil and, like she says, when it comes to doing the right thing—Honey goes where she is needed.

Harry Moon

Harry is Honey's older brother. He is thirteen years old and in the eighth grade at Sleepy Hollow Middle School. Harry is a magician. And not just a kid magician who does kid tricks, nope, Harry has the true gift of magic.

Harvest Moon

Harvest is the baby of the Moon family. He is two years old. Sometimes Honey has to watch him, but she mostly doesn't mind.

Mary Moon

Mary Moon is the mom. She is fair and straightforward with her kids. She loves them dearly, and they know it. Mary works full time as a nurse, so she often relies on her family for help around the house.

John Moon

John is the dad. He's a bit of a nerd. He works as an IT professional, and sometimes he thinks he would love it if his children followed in his footsteps. But he respects that Harry, Honey, and possibly Harvest will need to go their own way. John owns a classic sports car he calls Emma.

Half Moon

Half Moon is the family dog. He is big and clumsy and has floppy ears. Half is pretty much your basic dog.

FRIENDS

Becky Young

Becky is Honey's best friend. They've known each other since pre-school. Becky is quiet and smart. She is an artist. She is loyal to Honey and usually lets Honey take the lead, but occasionally, Becky makes her thoughts known. And she has really great ideas.

Claire Sinclair

Claire is also Honey's friend. She's a bit bossy, like Honey, so they sometimes clash. Claire is an athlete. She enjoys all sports but especially soccer, softball, and basketball. Sometimes kids poke fun at her rhyming name. But she doesn't mind—not one bit.

FOES

Clarice Maxine Kligore

Clarice is Honey's arch nemesis. For some reason Clarice doesn't like Honey and tries to bully her. But Honey has no trouble standing up to her. The reason Clarice likes to hassle Honey probably has something to do with the fact that Honey knows the truth abut the Kligores. They are evil.

Maximus Kligore

The Honorable (or not-so-honorable depending on your viewpoint) Maximus Kligore is the mayor of Sleepy Hollow. He is the one who plunged Sleepy Hollow into a state of eternal Halloween. He said it was just a publicity stunt to raise town revenues and increase jobs. But Honey knows differently. She knows there is more to Kligore's plans—something so much more sinister.

V

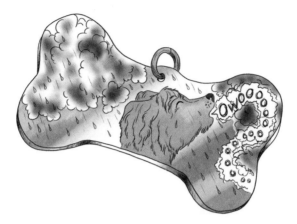

A HOWLING
IN THE NIGHT

The wind howled. Lightning crackled and rain poured sideways on Sleepy Hollow, Massachusetts. Honey Moon sat at her bedroom desk and looked out the window at her neighborhood. The rain was falling so hard, her view was blurred. She could barely make out the streetlights and houses.

On a clear night, Honey could see all the

way to the town green, a large park in the middle of town made famous by the bronze statue of the Headless Horseman from Washington Irving's scary story. The statue, standing more than fourteen feet tall, was the most sought after tourist attraction in all of Sleepy Hollow.

Yet, Honey thought she heard something off in the distance. A sound like howling. Sad and alone. But it wasn't the usual sounds of Sleepy Hollow where every day is Halloween night and where mournful cries and scary surprises lurked around every corner and in every shop and business.

No, this sound was different. She tried to ignore it by reading her book, but the sound seemed to pierce her heart, and she just couldn't stand it one second longer. She glanced at her turtle-shaped backpack. It had been a Christmas gift, and she hated it—at first. The turtle seemed so childish with its bright, neon-green shell and silly, googly eyes. But Honey also knew that this particular backpack was not ordinary. The more she carried it the more like a friend it became.

2

She could talk to Turtle.

"What should I do, Turtle?" Honey asked.

Honey waited and then, in a flash, she knew. She had to go out into the storm and find the source of the howling. The thought frightened her at first, but the more she looked at Turtle the more she knew she had to go, and she would be all right.

Honey pulled on her rain boots and jacket. She plopped a bright blue rain hat on her head and headed down the hallway determined to find the source of the sound. But before she could make it out into the dark, she was stopped.

"Honey Moon, where do you think you're going?"

Her mom stood at the bottom of the steps, arms crossed. She tapped one foot—a signal that she was upset or angry. "It's pouring rain. There's lightning. You can't go out."

3

"But, Mom," Honey said. "I have to. Don't you hear that howling? I need to find out what it is."

Honey's mom took a deep breath. "Probably just good old Sleepy Hollow. Nothing to worry about. This town seems to always have strange sounds."

Honey shook her head. "I don't think so, Mom. I think something or someone needs my help, and you know I always go where I am needed. And believe me, I am needed."

"Wait until the storm passes. Or for morning."

"But what if whatever it is . . . is hurt? I can't wait."

"Okay, fine," said Honey's mom. "But I'm going with you. We'll take the van. Just to be safe."

"Great," Honey said. "Let's go."

Honey and her mom climbed into the minivan. It was raining so hard, they were both soaking wet by the time they got the doors open. Honey didn't mind. "Come on, Mom, start the engine. Whatever it is needs me."

As Honey's mom pulled out of the driveway, Honey cracked her window just a tiny bit. The howling grew louder. And louder. And louder.

"I hear it now," Honey's mom said. She drove in the direction of the sound.

"I think it's coming from the green," Honey said.

She was correct. Honey's mom pulled the van up to the curb and opened her window just a little. The howling sound was loud and close.

"It's coming from the statue," Honey said. "Let's go."

"Hold on," Honey's mom said. "Not so quick. If it's coming from that infernal statue, it could be something . . . well, something evil. Especially on a night like this."

"But I can't just sit here," Honey said. "I have to go. I have to be brave."

Honey slid open the van door. She jumped out. "Come on, Mom, we'll be okay."

Together, Honey and her mom walked slowly toward the Headless Horseman. A bolt of lightning crackled overhead making Honey practically jump into her mother's arms.

"Are you sure about this? Maybe we should turn back," Mary Moon said.

"I'm sure," Honey said. "It just surprised me, that's all."

Honey sloshed through the saturated grass. Her boots squeaked with each step. Rain ran off the brim of her hat.

"There," Honey called. She ran. "It's right there."

Honey took a couple more steps toward the sound. And then she saw it. A dark, lumpy, shadowy thing cowered against the base of the statue. It shivered. It howled.

"Oh, Mom," Honey said. "It's a dog."

Honey knelt and stretched her hand toward the animal. "It's okay. I'm not gonna hurt you."

"Careful," Mary Moon said. "She could bite."

But the dog cowered and tried its best to push closer to the statue. Lightning cracked and for a quick second Honey saw the dog's eyes. They were sad. Honey swallowed. "It's okay, doggie."

Honey's mom knelt next to Honey. "She's so frightened."

"I know," Honey said. "We can't just leave her here."

"I know." Honey's mom reached toward the dog, but the dog pulled back.

Honey reached out her hand again. This time she was able to touch under the dog's chin. "Good doggie. See, I'm your friend."

"No collar," Honey said, looking at her mom. "A stray. We need to take her home and out of the storm."

"But how can we get her to come with us?

She's so scared."

Honey moved even closer. This time she was able to pat the dog's side and head. "It's okay. It's okay. We're gonna take you home where it's warm and safe."

More lightning cracked overhead. The dog shuddered and leaned into the statue.

Honey wrapped her arms around the dog. "I'm just gonna carry you to the car."

9

"Careful," Honey's mom said. "Don't let her bite you."

"Oh, she won't." Honey lifted the sopping, wet dog into her arms. She sloshed through the grass and mud. The dog felt a little heavy, but that was okay. Honey didn't mind. She didn't even mind that her coat and pants were covered with mud.

Honey's mom opened the van door. Honey gently set the dog down and then climbed into the back with her.

"Okay, let's go home and get the dog warmed up and dry," Mary Moon said.

On the way home, the dog rested her head in Honey's lap. Honey patted her head. "Good doggie. Good girl."

It wasn't long before Honey's mom pulled into the driveway.

Honey helped the dog out of the car. "Let's go inside. Mom? Will you get a fire going?"

"Fire?" Mary Moon said. "But it's summer."

"It's still chilly. Good old Sleepy Hollow. It's always autumn."

"You're right. You get a towel, a yucky towel, not one of my good ones, and dry her off good."

"Come on girl, let's go," Honey said. She was delighted when the dog walked right along with her. "Look, Mom, she likes me."

Honey's mom pushed open the front door. Honey and the little stray followed her inside. Honey was not expecting her little brother, two-year-old Harvest, to be there. He immediately squealed with delight.

"Doggie. Doggie."

"Careful, Harvest," Honey said. "She's a little scared. Don't get too close."

That was when Honey's dad dashed into the living room from the den. "What on earth?"

11

"Now, now, John," Honey's mom said. "She's a stray. She needed our help. And what is Harvest doing still up?"

Honey's dad tilted his head and smiled. "We were having fun playing hide and seek."

Honey wiped the dog's fur while her mom started the fire. "We have to let her stay, Dad," she said.

"Okay, okay," Honey's dad said. "Just don't

let Half Moon see her."

Honey looked around for the family dog. "Where is Half?"

"Harry's room," said John Moon.

"Good. Maybe he should stay there."

"John," said Honey's mom, "will you get Harvest into bed? I'm gonna make some chicken and rice for the dog. She's probably starved."

12

It wasn't long before the little dog was cuddling with Honey near the roaring fire. The sound of thunder and lightning still echoed overhead, and the rain still poured, but Honey felt good that she had rescued the dog. And now Honey could finally get a good look at the pooch. She wasn't a very big dog, certainly not as big as a golden retriever, and she wasn't small like a dachshund. She was more medium size with long, silver-gray fur. Her ears folded over at the tips. But she had bright eyes, and she didn't smell too bad for a dog that had been lost in the rain. All in all, Honey thought the stray gave off a good vibe.

Honey looked into the dog's eyes. "I think I'll call you Stormy since we found you on such a stormy night."

Honey saw her mom and dad exchange one of their "uh oh, we've got a problem" looks.

"Now, you know we can't keep her," Honey's dad said. "Don't get attached."

Honey patted Stormy's head and scratched her behind the ears. "I know. But everyone deserves a name—even if it only sticks for a little while."

"Okay," Honey's mom said. "Tomorrow we'll bring her to the Sleepy Hollow Animal Shelter."

Honey patted Stormy's head. She felt a twinge of sadness but also joy. It was the best thing, and since the Sleepy Hollow Animal Shelter was a no-kill shelter, she knew Stormy would find a great forever home.

14

Two Dogs, Now

Early the next morning, before first light, Honey crept down the stairs with her blanket wrapped around her shoulders. Stormy was cuddled in a blanket also, near the still warm fireplace.

"Hey, girl," Honey whispered. "It's just me."

Stormy poked her head up but didn't say a word.

"I thought you might be lonely." Honey lay down next to Stormy. "Mom wouldn't let you sleep in my bed because you still smell kind of awful. That's what she said; I don't think you smell *that* bad."

The rain had finally ended, and after a few minutes, the only sound Honey heard was Stormy snoring. Honey was having a little trouble falling asleep, but that was okay. It was nearly time for her parents to get up and start the day. Now that it was summer vacation, Honey liked to sleep late. But not today. Today she was going to take Stormy to the shelter, and that was both a good and a sad thing.

Honey yawned several times and tried to get as comfortable as possible. Stormy would move only slightly, and Honey didn't want to disturb her by moving around too much.

Soon, Honey heard noises upstairs. She heard the bathroom door close and the shower turn on.

16

"Oh, good," she whispered. "They're up."

With that, Stormy scrambled to her feet. Her tail wagged. Stormy wasn't a very big dog, but she was quite hairy. "I didn't mean for you to get up," Honey said with a laugh. But Stormy seemed to want something.

"I bet you need to go out."

But before Honey could stand up, Half Moon

bounded down the steps with Harry following behind.

"Gangway," Harry called. "Half Moon needs to go out."

Half Moon dashed into the living room, probably headed for the kitchen and the back door but came to a screeching halt the instant he saw Stormy. He sat on his brown haunches and looked at Honey and then growled at the strange dog. Stormy growled back and let out a loud bark.

"It's okay, girl. It's just Half Moon, our dumb dog."

"Hey," Harry said. "He's not dumb. He's just protective. Mom told me about the dog you found."

"Yeah, we're taking her to the shelter this morning."

Half Moon barked and growled.

"Good idea. I better get Half outside." Harry took Half Moon by the collar and led him into the kitchen.

"Come on, Stormy," Honey said. "We better go out the front." Honey had found one of Half's old collars and leashes, which worked just fine for Stormy. Honey walked into the yard with the pooch. She checked her pocket for a poop bag, which she fortunately had because she needed to use it pretty much right away. Then she walked toward the garage and tossed the bag in the trash. "Good girl, Stormy," she said. "I wish we could keep you."

But Honey knew that would be impossible. Sometimes having one dog was a big enough chore, and when it came right down to it, Honey really did love Half Moon—even if he was a big, old klutz and mostly Harry's dog.

Honey led Stormy out onto the sidewalk. The air was already warm but not quite as humid as yesterday, now that the storm had passed. She took a deep breath of the Sleepy Hollow air that always seemed to smell like

19

autumn even in July. As she walked, she wondered where Stormy came from and why she was lost.

"Maybe your owners are looking for you," she said. "Do you know where you live?"

But Stormy only walked on, stopping every few seconds to sniff the grass or paw around a hydrant or electrical pole. Honey hoped Stormy might be able to sniff her way home, but she also knew that most likely she and her mom would be taking her to the shelter this morning.

Honey had been to the shelter a few times—just to visit the dogs. Most of the time she felt sad seeing the pooches in their kennels but also glad that they had been rescued.

When she returned home, Honey's mom was in the kitchen scrambling eggs. Bacon was sizzling in the pan, and Harry was setting the table. Stormy must have smelled the bacon because she barked once and whined a little. Then she sat down and lifted her paws in the air like she was begging.

"Look," Honey said. "She is such a smart dog. Half Moon has lived here practically his whole life, and all he can do is roll over and cause calamity."

"He can do more than that," Harry said. But just as the words left his mouth, Half Moon came bounding into the kitchen. He stopped short and slid, rear end first, into his food and water bowls. Stormy barked once and then gave Honey a look that said, "Is he always like this?"

"Harry," said Mary Moon, "grab some paper towels and clean that up and then pour more kibble in his dish. And you better set a bowl out for Stormy too."

"I'll do it," Honey said. "I mean I'll get Stormy some kibble."

Honey poured kibble into a yellow bowl and placed it on the floor—far away from Half Moon's spot. Stormy had no trouble gulping the food down and lapping at the water. Honey

21

thought she looked so appreciative that she couldn't help but give her a big squeeze around the neck.

"Awww, do we have to take her to the shelter?" Honey asked with a little bit of pleading in her voice.

Mary Moon turned her attention from the eggs. "I'm afraid so, dear. We just can't have two dogs."

Honey squeezed the lost dog tighter. "Well, I'm going to love her all I can before she has to leave."

Mary Moon spooned eggs onto Honey's and Harry's plates. She dropped three strips of bacon onto each plate as well. "And don't worry," she said. "I saved a piece for Stormy and Half Moon."

"Good," Honey said. "I was going to share, but it's good to know I don't have to now."

Harry laughed. "Yeah, me too."

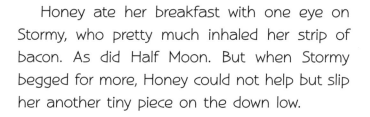

Honey ate her breakfast with one eye on Stormy, who pretty much inhaled her strip of bacon. As did Half Moon. But when Stormy begged for more, Honey could not help but slip her another tiny piece on the down low.

Mary Moon sat at the table. She held a mug of coffee, which she sipped slowly while Harry and Honey ate. When they finished, she said, "So I guess we should get to the shelter as soon as it opens."

23

Honey looked at her plate. Sad feelings swelled inside, and she felt a tear form in her right eye. It would be hard to let the dog go.

Harry carried his plate to the dishwasher. "It was a good thing you did, sis," he said. "I still don't know how you were able to hear her through the storm."

"I know," Honey said as she swallowed the last of her eggs. "It was kind of faint at first, and then it got a little louder. I thought it was the wind, but then something inside of me said it wasn't and that I needed to investigate, and you know how I am when it comes to a mystery—I have to solve it."

"Good job," Harry said. He hoisted his backpack onto his shoulders. "I gotta run. I'm meeting the Good Mischief Team. We need to talk about ways to raise a little cash this summer."

"Okay," Mary Moon said. "Have fun."

Harry kissed his mother's cheek. "It's business. Not fun."

Honey carried her dish to the sink, rinsed it, and placed it into the dishwasher. Then she sat back down at the table. "I wish I could find a way to make some cash this summer."

Honey's mom pulled her mug from her lips. "Maybe you can. Odd jobs and such around town."

Honey shrugged, "I guess. But I just wish there was something more important I could do."

"Well, helping someone with their chores is pretty important," Mary said.

Honey patted Stormy's head. "Come on, girl. We better get ready to go."

"Hold on," Honey's mom said. "I think maybe we should give Stormy a bath first. She's pretty yucky."

Honey looked down at Stormy. Stormy looked up at Honey and whimpered. "You're right," Honey said. "She could definitely use a bath. I can do it outside like I do with Half Moon."

"Use that galvanized bucket out there and use Half's shampoo," Mary Moon said.

"Okay. Come on, Stormy, time for your bath."

Honey hooked the leash on the small fence that surrounded the back patio. Then she grabbed the hose and filled the large bucket with water. Next, she had to get Stormy into the bucket. Usually, when she washed Half, she just let him sit on the concrete patio. But Stormy was so dirty she needed a little extra attention.

"Come on, get in," Honey said. But Stormy just sat there. "Now, girl, let's go. Jump in."

But still, Stormy did not budge.

So Honey picked her up and set her in the water. Stormy shook like mad and stepped out of the bucket. Honey pushed her back in. Stormy climbed out again. Honey pushed her back in. "Come on, Stormy. Please stay. You really need this bath."

This time, Honey held her in place and used the hose to soak Stormy's fur. Finally, Stormy sat still and let Honey rub her body with the sweet-smelling shampoo.

"Doesn't that feel good?" Honey said as the shampoo lathered and bubbled all over Stormy. Honey laughed. "You look like a polar bear. Well, maybe."

Honey finished Stormy's bath and rinsed her

off. After she wiped Stormy down with some towels, she cleaned up the porch and said, "I better go change now. I'm covered with dog water."

Stormy followed Honey upstairs and into her room. The now clean dog flopped onto the colorful, circular rug on the floor. "Hey," Honey said. "You even have some white fur on your chest. Couldn't see it before with all the dirt." Honey snapped a few pictures on her phone.

27

Stormy let out a few whimpers that seemed to sink directly into Honey's heart. Letting Stormy go was going to be the hardest thing ever.

28

A Most Brilliant Idea

Summer was always Honey's favorite time of the year. Even though she loved school and was a great student, she loved the freedom summer brought. And this year was no different, except now she thought it might be time to look for a little job, and Stormy gave her a brilliant idea. An idea that would not only help Honey earn some cash but provided a service as well.

So on the way to the shelter Honey said,

"You know, Mom, I was thinking. Maybe I could start a dog-walking service."

Harvest giggled when Stormy licked his hand.

At first, Honey thought she heard her mother let out a little chuckle also. But then her mom said, "Really? Are you sure? That's a lot of responsibility."

"Oh, I know that," Honey said. "But I can start slow. Maybe just two or three dogs and then build it up. Who knows? I might even have to add a few employees at some point. I can be an entrepreneur."

Mary Moon turned onto Magic Row. The shelter was located just a few blocks down. "I guess you could try. You'll have to advertise, and you know, Honey, you have to clean up after them—even the big dogs, especially the big dogs."

"Mom, I clean up after Half Moon, and he can do some amazing—"

30

"All right, all right, Honey, I guess you can give it a try."

Honey looked through the window at the passing businesses on Magic Row. Some new businesses had moved in, like the Bootique, but mostly the businesses had been there for a long, long time, like Chillie Willies costume shop, which Mayor Kligore owned. His son, Titus, the big bully of Sleepy Hollow, usually worked there all summer. And some of the kids around town got jobs at the other stores or mowed lawns or ran errands. But Honey thought her idea was the best one yet. She was sure to make a lot of money.

"I wonder," she thought out loud. "How much should I charge?"

"Not too much at first," Mary Moon said as she pulled into the animal shelter parking lot. "You want to build business and gain people's confidence first. Taking care of someone's pet carries a lot of weight."

"Uhm, you're right, Mom. I need to prove that

31

I can handle the job."

Stormy barked three times. Honey thought she was approving of her plan. But then the sad feelings returned. It was time to say goodbye.

Honey slid open the side door, and Stormy hopped out. Honey secured the leash around her wrist and hand. Good practice.

32

"Come on, girl," Honey said. "And don't worry. Someone will adopt a good-looking dog like you real quick."

Honey swallowed. She hoped she was correct. The thought of Stormy sitting in a kennel for a long time was hard to bear.

Honey walked toward the entrance of the small building. It was constructed of brick and wood with an orange shingle roof. The barks and howls of the dogs sheltered inside grew louder the closer she got.

Mary Moon pulled open the door, and Honey

and Stormy walked inside. There was a woman sitting behind a counter with a phone and a computer monitor and stacks of green folders on it. She seemed tall to Honey even though she was sitting down. She had blond hair pulled into a ponytail and wore turquoise glasses. She was also wearing a gray shirt with Sleepy Hollow Animal Shelter embroidered over the pocket and the name Terry embroidered under that. A small embroidered puppy with long, floppy ears was curled under her name. Honey thought it was a basset hound, and she also figured the woman's name was Terry—not the puppy.

33

She looked down at Stormy. "Here we go, Stormy. But don't worry. This is a good place."

"Hi, my name is Terry. Can I help you?" the woman asked.

Honey looked up at her mom who nodded and smiled. "Yes," Honey said. "I found this dog last night—during the storm. We can't keep her."

Terry stood. Honey was right; she was tall.

She leaned over the counter and looked at Stormy. "What a sweet doggie. You say you found her?"

"Yes," Mary Moon said. "We found her at the park near the statue. We think she's a stray or might be lost."

"I think so too," Terry said. "So you want to surrender her?"

"Surrender?" Honey said. "Wow, no, we just want you to find her a good forever home."

Terry smiled widely. "Oh, that's just what we call it when someone gives us their dog."

"Well, she's not really our dog. We just found her."

"I understand." Terry sat back down and tapped the keyboard. "I just need some information, and then we'll take the dog back to our isolation section.

"Isolation?" Honey said. She sounded alarmed

as she petted Stormy's silver-gray fur. "Why?"

"It's standard procedure for all strays and surrenders. Just to make sure they're not ill or have other problems."

"Oh, well, Stormy is fine. Not ill and she has no problems—other than needing a family."

That was when Stormy let out a sneeze. Terry looked at Honey.

35

"Just allergies. She didn't sneeze the whole time we had her."

"And how long is that?" Terry asked.

"Just since last night. I heard her howling during the storm, and we went out and found her in the town green, near the Headless Horseman statue. She was wet and scared."

"I'll bet," Terry said.

Terry took some more information and then took hold of Stormy's leash. "I guess that will be all. I'll just take her back."

Honey felt tears well up inside. "Oh no, can I . . . can I please walk back with you to say goodbye?"

"Sure. Come on."

"I'll be back, Mom."

Honey followed Terry through the double doors and down a short corridor. "She won't be alone," she said. "There are two other doggies in isolation."

"That's good," Honey said as she swiped away some tears. "Please find her a good home. A place with kids."

"We'll do our best, and remember, this is a no-kill shelter. She'll stay as long as it takes, and she's so cute I don't think it will take long at all."

Honey smiled and let out a breath she had been holding. "That's good to hear."

Just then, a girl, about Honey's age, walked out from another room. She was kind of tall and skinny and wore a blue smock.

"Hi," Honey said.

The girl looked at Honey and then knelt down and patted Stormy. "Hi. She is so cute."

"I know," Honey replied.

37

The girl stood. Terry handed her the leash. "This is Isabela Bonito; she volunteers here."

"Cool," Honey said.

"It's kind of my thing. I love all dogs and cats but mostly dogs."

"You can put Stormy in kennel three," Terry told Isabela. "I'll be back to sign her in and stuff in a few minutes."

"Okay," Isabela replied.

Honey hugged Stormy. "Don't worry," she said through tears. "You are going to get the best home ever. I just know it, and I'll come visit every day until that happens."

"Don't worry," Isabela said. "She will be fine. I'll take good care of her."

Isabela gave a little tug on Stormy's leash, and Honey watched as Isabela and Stormy disappeared behind a closed door.

THE SLEEPY HOLLOW HOWLERS

Honey wanted to be quiet on the way home. It was time to try and put Stormy in the back of her mind and concentrate on her new dog-walking business. *Think. Think. Think.*

"You'll have to advertise," her mom said as though she was reading Honey's mind. But moms can be like that. "Maybe a sign at the pet store."

"Great idea. Thanks. I'll ask Becky to help. She's such a good artist, and maybe she can even go into business with me."

Mary Moon nodded. "I like that plan, Honey Moon. And I think I would feel better knowing you had a friend walking dogs with you."

"Will you drop me off at Becky's?"

"Sure, sounds good."

Honey tapped her cell and sent Becky a text. "R U hme? Can I come ovr?"

About two seconds later Honey's phone chimed. "Sure."

"Great, Mom, she's home. I know she's gonna be really excited about the business."

Honey's mom pulled the van alongside the curb in front of Becky's house. Becky was already outside and waving.

40

"See ya later," Honey said as she jumped out of the van.

"Be home for supper," Mary Moon called.

Honey waved and then headed up the driveway past all of Becky's mom's whirligigs and other lawn art. Becky's mom was an artist who specialized in country crafts like whirligigs and mailboxes. That's where Becky got her talent. "Becky," Honey called. "You won't believe what just happened and have I got the best idea ever."

41

"What?" Becky called. "What happened?"

Honey followed Becky onto the porch. They sat on the swing that hung from the porch roof.

"Last night, during the storm, I found a dog."

"A dog? In the storm? Where?"

"Near old scary horseface."

Becky laughed. Then Honey told her the

whole story about Stormy.

"Look," Honey said as she took her phone from her pocket. "This is her."

"Oh, she's adorable," Becky said.

Honey saved her best news for last. "And that's when I got the idea for a business."

"A business? What kind?"

"A dog-walking service. We can offer to walk dogs for people while they're at work or busy or when they just don't want to. I'm sure people will pay us."

"That does sound like a good idea," Becky said. But then her face grew sad.

"What's wrong?" Honey asked.

43

"I was just thinking about Stormy at the shelter. It makes me sad."

Honey leaped off the swing. "Hey, maybe you can adopt her."

Becky shook her head. "No way. My dad is allergic."

"Awww, that's too bad. Well, you can come visit her with me. I promised I would visit every day until she found a forever home."

"That sounds good. Can we go today?"

"Sure, but we better get started on our business first."

"Right. What do we do?"

"Well, we start by advertising. We can hang a sign at the pet store. I figure you can make the sign."

"Come on," Becky said. "To the craft room." She always jumped at any idea that required her artistic talents.

Honey followed Becky into her house. Becky's mom was sitting at the dining room table surrounded by papers. "Bills," she said. "Ugh."

Honey laughed. "Yeah, my dad gets that look every month too."

Mrs. Young rifled through a pile of pages. "Where is that electric bill?"

"Come on, Honey," Becky said. "Let's go work on the business. We'll tell Mom later."

44

Honey and Becky climbed the steps to the second floor. The craft room was the most spectacular room in Becky's house. It was really an extra bedroom they converted into a studio. There were crafts tables and bins and cabinets chock-full of pretty much every single art supply anyone could imagine. Spools of bright ribbons hung from peg boards. There was even a large cardboard box filled with old wallpaper scraps— some of them were pretty fancy.

Becky sat on one of the stools at the long craft table. "So where do we start?"

45

Honey scratched her head. "Let me think. Well, the first thing we need is a name."

"Good idea. How about B & H Dog Walking?"

"B? How come you go first?"

"It's alphabetical."

Honey shook her head. "But it was my idea, so it should be H & B Dog Walking."

"Let's come up with something that doesn't include our names."

"Good idea," Honey said. "It probably should sound Sleepy Holloweeeeeennnny."

Becky pulled the lid off a bright green marker. "Uhm, what could it be?"

"It needs to be catchy, something people will remember and recognize right away." Honey tapped a pencil on the table while Becky tapped her forehead. *Think. Think. Think.*

Honey snapped her fingers. "I got it! It was Stormy's howling that led me to her, so why don't we call our business Sleepy Hollow Howlers?"

"Sleepy Hollow Howlers." Becky tapped her finger on her chin. "I like it."

"Good, I like it too. I think people will notice the name and get curious."

"Now we need a good poster."

"Right, and use both our cell numbers."

Becky started to draw on a sketch book. She drew dogs sitting and standing and rolling over. She drew dogs barking and wagging their tails, but when she drew a dog howling at a full moon, she and Honey knew that was the perfect picture.

"I love it," Honey said. She jumped off the stool and snagged a piece of poster board from a stack on the floor. "Use this," she said. "It needs to be big."

47

"But not too big," Becky said. "Let's cut that in half."

Honey pulled a pair of scissors from the ribbon peg board. The Youngs had nine different kinds of scissors, some with different edges on the blades. A pair that cut crinkles, a pair that cut waves, and even a pair that had five separate blades for cutting fringes.

Becky expertly cut the poster board down the middle. "That's better," she said. Then she wrote The Sleepy Hollow Howlers in wide, bright, neon-green letters. She added their cell numbers and wrote, "Call today!" Then she held it up. Honey read all the words three times to make sure everything was spelled correctly. No problem.

But Becky wasn't quite finished. She drew a squiggly line all around the edge and then used pink glitter glue to make paw prints all around the business name.

"It's spectacular," Honey said. "We're sure to get business with this."

"Come on. Let's go to the pet shop."

"I hope Miss Muffet lets us hang it up."

"Why wouldn't she?"

Honey shrugged and then she and Becky dashed down the steps and out the door.

"We are going to have the best business ever," Honey said.

"We'll be rich," Becky said with a grin.

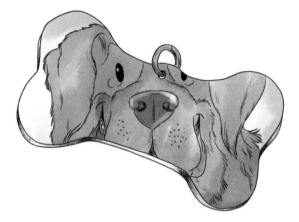

A VERY BIG FIRST CLIENT

Honey and Becky stood outside Hocus Pocus Pets. It was the only pet store in Sleepy Hollow and definitely the best place to advertise, but Becky was all of a sudden feeling nervous about asking if they could hang their sign.

"What if Miss Muffet asks us a bunch of questions? Do we need a license or anything?"

Honey shrugged. "We're ten years old. We aren't old enough for a license. It'll be fine, and if we need permission or something, we'll get it."

"Okay," Becky said. "Here we go."

Honey pulled open the door. A bell jingled. She looked around at the bright store. She saw bird cages hanging from the ceiling and doggie beds piled high in a corner. There was a shelf stocked with different dog and cat foods and an aisle dedicated only to pet toys.

"Wow," Honey said. "Look at all this stuff. I never really noticed before. I mean we come here a lot to get Half Moon stuff but—"

"But what?" Becky asked.

"It's just that I think we should be glad that even our pets are taken care of so well." She thought about the little girl from India her family sponsored. Honey and her mom sent a check every month just so she could go to school and have fresh water. Her name was Anisha, and she sometimes had to work in the fields and fetch water from more than a mile away from her home.

Honey looked around the shop. An orange cat was curled in the window. His name was Boris. Miss Muffet named him after a famous, old-timey movie actor. Honey couldn't keep from giving Boris a scratch behind the ear. Boris loved it.

"I think we should donate some of our earnings to a good cause," Honey said.

"Good idea," Becky said. "Like that girl you sponsor."

"Exactly," Honey said. "That's just what I was thinking." Now she was even more excited about her business. Not only would they get fun money but they would be doing something important that would help Anisha.

Honey straightened her shoulders and practically marched up to the counter. Miss Muffet, a kind of small woman who always wore black and a hat with bat ears, smiled. Honey smiled back, ignoring Miss Muffet's costume. And it was just a costume. Honey had seen her plenty of times around town wearing normal clothes; although, she was wearing the bat ears at the grocery store.

"Miss Muffet," Honey said. "My friend Becky and I are starting a dog-walking service and—"

"Oh, that is glorious," Miss Muffet said. "A young couple was just in here looking for a dog walker. They're new to town."

Honey and Becky looked at each. "Really?" they said together.

"Yes," Miss Muffet said. "I have their name and address right here."

Miss Muffet gave Honey the yellow sticky note.

"Wow, thank you," Honey said. "But would it be all right if we hung our sign for advertising in your fine shop?"

"Of course," Miss Muffet said. "Why don't you put it right in the front window, and I'll be sure to mention you to anyone else who might be looking for a dog walker."

"Thank you," Honey and Becky said politely.

Miss Muffet gave Honey a roll of tape, and Honey secured their sign to the front window while Becky ran outside to make sure it was in the perfect spot for the best visibility.

Becky gave Honey a thumbs-up.

Honey returned the tape and said, "Thank you. I think we'll go right over to—" She looked at the sticky note, "To the Stevenses' house."

53

"Good idea," Miss Muffet said.

Honey was so excited that when she dashed past the dog bed display, she slipped a little and went crashing into the soft mountain. The beds tumbled down all around with one bed landing smack-dab on her head. A couple of customers laughed a little before asking if she was okay.

Honey laughed. She scrambled to her feet. "I am so sorry," she said. "I'll help you stack them."

Becky was laughing too hard to say anything.

"It's okay," Miss Muffet. "I'll fix it. It was kind of precarious anyway."

Honey smiled. "I'm sorry, and believe me, I'm usually not this clumsy."

"I hope so," Miss Muffet said. "Dog walkers need some steady feet."

"Oh, I am very steady. I walk Half Moon all the time, and he's a big, oafy klutz himself."

"It runs in the family," Becky said. She grabbed Honey's hand. "Come on, we better go."

Becky and Honey dashed down Broom Stick Drive and rounded the corner onto Skeleton Street. Honey stopped and checked the note. "They live at two hundred and twenty-two."

"That's it, over there." Becky pointed to a white house with a gray porch and red roof, a pretty typical house in Sleepy Hollow.

54

"Look," Honey said. "The dog is in the yard."

"Wowzers, what kind of dog is that?"

"It's a Saint Bernard, and he is huge."

Honey watched Becky's eyes grow as big as tea cup saucers. "We can't walk that . . . that beast."

"Sure we can," Honey said. "I bet he's as gentle as can be. Most really big dogs are.

Come on, let's go talk to the Stevenses."

They crossed the street and stood near the Stevenses' fenced yard. The dog was sitting still, not moving a muscle.

"See," Honey said. "He's gentle. Isn't he cute?"

But just as the words left her mouth, the dog let out a loud, deep bark that knocked Honey right back to the curb. Becky grabbed hold of her arm. "Uhm, maybe we shouldn't do this."

"Nonsense," Honey said as she regained her balance. "He's just protecting his home."

She walked up to the front gate. This time the large black, white, and tan dog moved slowly toward her. His wide jowls hung down. Slobber dripped from his lips.

"Oh dear," Becky said. "He's a mess."

"Awwww, he's just a dog," Honey said. She reached her hand over the gate. The dog settled on his haunches, and his head still

reached higher than the fence. Honey patted his head.

"See," she said. "He likes me now."

That was when the front door opened. Honey figured it was Mrs. Stevens standing on the porch. She waved. Mrs. Stevens waved back.

"Here, Bart," called Mrs. Stevens. "Come here, boy."

The dog bounded up the porch steps.

57

"Can I help you?" Mrs. Stevens called.

"Yes," Honey called. "Miss Muffet at the pet store said you were looking for a dog walker."

A wide smile burst across the woman's face. "Yes, we are," Mrs. Stevens said. "Come on up."

Honey and Becky smiled at each other. "Here we go," Honey said. "Our first client."

58

VISITING THE SHELTER

I t didn't take long for Mrs. Stevens to hire Sleepy Hollow Howlers to walk her 180-pound Saint Bernard. Mrs. Stevens assured them that even though he was quite heavy, Bart walked well on the leash.

"He's big," she had said. "But he's such a good boy."

Honey had to admit she was a little nervous, but after Mrs. Stevens suggested a trial run and it went pretty well, Honey was convinced they could handle the big pooch. And besides, he was probably the cutest dog Honey had ever seen, other than Stormy, of course, and Half Moon. Bart was a gentle and sweet giant.

So it was settled. Honey and Becky would come to the Stevenses' house the next morning at nine o'clock and take Bart for a walk. Mrs. Stevens made sure the Howlers knew where the pooper-scooper and bags were. And since she would not be home, she showed Honey and Becky where they kept an extra house key.

The Howlers patted Bart on the head. He gave them a hearty woof and off the Howlers went to get ready for their first big dog-walking day.

"Can you believe it?" Honey said as they walked toward her house. "We already have a client."

"I know. And a big one. Let's go to my house. I want to tell my mom."

"Okay, but can we stop by the shelter first? I want to check on Stormy."

"That's right. I almost forgot. Let's go. I can't wait to meet her."

The walk to the shelter was a little long but not so bad. Bikes would have been a better idea, but the day was so warm and nice that walking was actually a pleasure if you didn't mind passing a bunch of creepy spider displays and plastic ravens on nearly every fence post. They walked past their friend Claire's house, but she was not home. Claire was spending part of her summer at her Aunt Beverly's house in Idaho.

"It's too bad Claire isn't here," Becky said. "She would love to be part of our business."

"Yeah," Honey said. "Maybe when she gets back. We'll probably have so many clients by then we'll really need her help."

Honey opened the shelter door. She was greeted by Terry, the same woman who was

there earlier.

"Hi," Terry said. "Back already?"

"Yes," Honey said. "I just wanted to check on Stormy."

"Oh, she's still in isolation, but she seems happy. Eating and playing. Isabela is taking real good care of her."

62

"Who is Isabela?" Becky asked.

"Oh she's a volunteer here," Honey said. "She was here this morning when we dropped Stormy off."

"Yep," Terry said. "Isabela has been taking real good care of her."

"Can we visit?" Honey asked.

Terry screwed up her face. "Well, not really. She's in isolation."

Honey looked down. "Oh, I understand."

"I have an idea," Terry said. "You can look at her through the door window. I just can't let you in the isolation wing."

"I understand," Honey said. "I just want to see her. And show her to Becky."

"Good," Terry said. She pressed a button on the counter. "Isabela will be out in a minute to take you back."

While they waited, Honey got a great idea. "Excuse me, Terry," she said. "Becky and I are professional dog walkers. Our business is called Sleepy Hollow Howlers—"

"Oh," Terry said. "I haven't heard of you."

"That's because we just got started today," Becky explained. "We have our first client."

"Oh, I see," Terry said. "That would explain it."

"Anyway," Honey said, looking around the lobby. "Would it be okay if we hung one of our

63

signs on that bulletin board over there?"

Terry looked like she was thinking. Then she said, "I guess so, but I need to check with the supervisor first."

"Okay," Becky replied. "I need to make another sign anyway."

"Come back tomorrow," Terry said.

64   And that was when Isabela appeared from the back. "Hi," she said. "I remember you."

"Hi," Honey said. "This is Becky. We came to visit Stormy."

"Oh, you can't," Isabela said.

"Actually," Terry interjected, "I told them they could look through the door."

"Cool, come on back."

Isabela led Honey and Becky to the isolation wing of the shelter. Fortunately, the door had a big glass window, and Honey could see Stormy pretty well. "Oh, look at her. She's so pretty," Honey said.

"I think she's my favorite stray this month," Isabela said. "I think she's got some collie and maybe German shepherd in her."

"Wow," Becky said. "She is adorable."

Stormy noticed them. She stood and barked.

"She's a great dog," Isabela said. "I wish I could keep her."

65

"Why don't you?" Honey asked.

Becky gave Honey a nudge.

Isabela shrugged. "It's okay. It's just that I don't even have a real home—yet. I live with a nice woman on the other side of town."

Honey swallowed. "I'm sorry about that."

"Don't be. It's a good home. The best one I've been in since . . . well, since I lost my parents."

Honey didn't know what to say. She just looked at Isabela and finally asked, "Where do you go to school?"

"I think I'll be going to Sleepy Hollow Elementary."

"Us too," Honey said. "That's great. You'll like it there."

"Good," Isabela said. "I like Sleepy Hollow."

66

Honey thought things were getting a little uncomfortable. She had never met anyone like Isabela before, and it was hard to know how to act. But Isabela made it a little easier.

"My foster home is really nice," she said. "And I like coming here. My foster mother, Nan Mapleleaf—great name, huh?—got me the job volunteering here. But I can really relate to the dogs, you know."

"Yeah," Honey said. "I guess, but don't you get sad?"

"For the dogs?"

Honey looked at Stormy again. "Well, the dogs and for yourself."

"Sometimes, but like I said, it's really not so bad."

That was when Becky piped up. "You can be our friend. You can hang out with us if that's okay with your mom . . . I mean your, uh . . . Nan."

67

Isabela laughed. "Sure. That would be great."

Honey liked the idea also. Then she told Isabela about the Sleepy Hollow Howlers, and Isabela gave her some pointers about walking dogs. "The most important tip," Isabela said, "is to try and stay in front or next to the dog. You have to be the alpha dog."

Honey laughed at Isabela's suggestion. So did Becky. In fact, Becky laughed so hard she got the dogs in the shelter barking wildly.

"Why are you laughing?" Isabela asked.

"Because our fist client is a 180-pound Saint Bernard. He weighs more than both of us put together."

Isabela smiled widely. "Oh wow! I love Saint Bernards."

"He is really sweet," Becky said.

"Yeah, he belongs to the new people who moved in on Skeleton Street."

Isabela shook her head. "Skeleton. Why is everything supposed to be so spooky around here? Nan tried to explain it to me. And I guess it's kind of cool. But I think Mayor Kligore gives me the creeps, even though I've never seen him. I live near Folly Farm, and I see long black cars driving on and off the property." She shivered. "It's creepy."

"Oh wow," Honey said. "I bet you've seen some odd things."

Isabela shook her head. "Just the cars, really. But just looking at the place makes me feel weird."

Honey and Becky explained all about Mayor Kligore and the Headless Horseman to Isabela. She thought it was kind of kooky but also kind of cool in a way.

"Always Halloween," she said. "Too bad we don't get candy every day."

Honey said goodbye to Stormy who, for a moment, seemed sad.

"She'll be okay," Isabela said. "I'll take good care of her."

70

A SPECIAL GIFT

I t had been a long day, and Honey was quite glad to get home and sit down to a big plate of spaghetti and meatballs. Honey's mom had come home early from her job as a nurse and made Honey's favorite meal. It was really Harry's favorite too, and Harvest loved to slurp spaghetti strings.

Honey had no trouble cleaning her plate. But not before she shared her news with

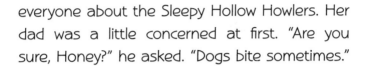

everyone about the Sleepy Hollow Howlers. Her dad was a little concerned at first. "Are you sure, Honey?" he asked. "Dogs bite sometimes."

"I'm sure," Honey said between spaghetti slurps. "And we already met our first dog, Bart. He's a Saint Bernard."

Harry laughed so hard he spat meatball across the table. "Seriously? You can't handle such a big dog. Stick to the Chihuahuas."

Honey smirked at him. "I can too handle him. We had a tryout at the Stevenses' house today; they're his owners."

Honey's mom wiped her mouth with a paper napkin and said, "I think she'll be just fine. Honey is a very strong girl."

"A regular Pippi Longstocking," her dad said. "But please, Honey, be careful."

"I will." Honey slurped a long spaghetti strand, which made Harvest laugh.

After she had eaten enough, she told them about Isabela at the shelter.

"Well, I, for one, think it is a great idea that you make her a friend," Mary Moon said.

"Me too," John Moon said.

Harvest dumped his spaghetti on the floor and laughed. Mary jumped up to get paper towels, but Half Moon had beaten her to it. He lapped the spaghetti up lickety-split.

"Oh, Half," Honey said. "I don't know if dogs should eat spaghetti."

It was Honey's turn to load the dishwasher. It wasn't the hardest chore in the world. She would rather do dishes than fold laundry any day. She had just finished when her eye caught the picture of Anisha, the little girl the family sponsored. It was on the refrigerator. "I'm glad we can help," she said, "and now with the Sleepy Hollow Howlers we'll be able to help even more."

"Who are you talking to," her mom asked.

Honey turned around. Her mom was standing at the kitchen doorway. "I thought I heard you talking."

"Oh," Honey said. "I guess I was, kind of." She dried her hands and placed the towel on the counter. "I was talking to Anisha. Becky and I are going to send her some of the money we make this summer."

Honey's mom took a step toward Honey. "Why, Honey Moon," she said with a huge smile, "I think that's a great idea. I am so proud of you."

Honey felt her face blush and get warm. "It's not much, Mom. But we have so much already. I want to share."

Mary Moon gave Honey a big hug. "You know, Honey, I think the organization we work with will let you earmark your donation for something special like a new desk or books."

Honey glanced at Anisha. "Really? Can we send her a desk? I remember in one of her letters she said it was hard to find a place to do homework—when she gets it."

"I think that's a splendid idea. Your dad and I will chip in also."

Honey took a deep breath. Dog walking was turning out to be the best idea she ever had.

Then Honey said, "But I wish I could help Isabela too. I mean she needs a forever home too."

"She does," Mary Moon said. "And I'm sure she'll get one. But from what you've told me about her, she seems to be doing pretty well."

Honey shrugged. "Yeah, she does seem happy, and I'm glad I can be her friend, it's just . . . just that I can't imagine what it must be like to not have a mom, a real mom."

Mary Moon pulled Honey close. "Neither can I."

That night Honey hung out in her room

reading and thinking about her new business. She sat at her desk and peered through the window at her town. Her thoughts kept turning to Isabela.

Turtle hung on the back of her chair. She kept feeling it nudge her back. Turtle was more than a backpack. Although she couldn't be certain, she did believe at times that he truly did have her back covered in more ways than one.

She reached around and snagged Turtle. "You can be so lumpy," she said.

Turtle didn't say anything, but Honey did get the sense that he wanted her to know something. When Honey was feeling low or had a problem to solve, Turtle was often whom she consulted. It was good to bounce things off a trusted friend.

77

"Did I do something wrong?" Honey asked.

No. She did not. What she did was something pretty sensational, and Turtle seemed to smile. But she couldn't be a hundred percent sure.

"Tomorrow is my first day of business. I don't want to mess up. And that Saint Bernard is pretty big."

She slipped the backpack over the chair and grabbed her diary. She opened to a fresh page and wrote:

> *More than anything I want*
> *to make enough money to get*
> *Anisha a desk. But I also want*
> *to have fun.*

Then she drew some doodle hearts and flowers until she figured out what she wanted to write next.

> *I also want to help Isabela.*
> *But I have no idea how to do that.*
> *Finding a home for a dog is one*
> *thing but a home for a person*
> *is another. I wish I could wave*
> *Harry's magic wand and POOF,*
> *she'd have a forever family.*

She felt Turtle dig into her back again. Not too hard but enough to remind her that he was there.

> *I guess I need to leave it up to*
> *the great Magician, as Harry*
> *would say.*

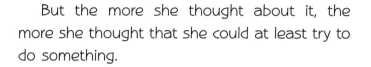

But the more she thought about it, the more she thought that she could at least try to do something.

80

THE COMPETITION

Morning arrived with rain pummeling the roof of Honey's house. Ugh. It was her first big dog-walking day, and now she had to contend with rain. Double ugh because Honey knew that probably meant a wet dog with dirty feet. And in this case, it meant wet Saint Bernard! Saint Bernard feet were as big as softballs.

But Honey also knew she had made a promise and commitment to the Stevenses.

She could not let the rain keep her from doing her job. She dressed quickly, choosing blue shorts and a yellow shirt. She pulled on a pair of neon-green, knee-high socks and headed downstairs.

Honey's mom was already in the kitchen getting ready to leave for work. Mrs. Wilcox was there also. She was Harvest's babysitter and pretty much a member of the family. Mrs. Wilcox used to babysit Honey.

"Morning," Honey said as she grabbed a box of Cheerios from the cupboard. "It's going to be a great day."

"Why, good morning, Honey," Mrs. Wilcox said. "You seem chipper today."

Honey patted Harvest, who was sitting in his booster seat at the table. "Good morning, little bro."

She sat at the table. "I am chipper. Even though it's raining cats and dogs."

Mrs. Wilcox pulled a Cheerio from Harvest's left ear. "How come? You have something exciting planned for the day?"

"I sure do," Honey said. "Today, I am starting my new business, Sleepy Hollow Howlers."

"Really? What are Sleepy Hollow Howlers?"

"It's the name of my new dog-walking business. Becky is doing it with me."

Honey's mom grabbed her backpack from the kitchen counter. "Honey is now Sleepy Hollow's newest entrepreneur."

"I'm impressed," Mrs. Wilcox said.

Honey poured milk over her Cheerios. "I kind of wish it wasn't raining, though."

"Just remember to wipe the dog's feet before you bring him back to the house," Mary Moon said.

"Oh, I know, Mom. Can I take a roll of

paper towels with me, just in case the Stevenses don't have any?"

"Good idea," Mary Moon said. "Now I have to get going. I can't be late."

Honey had just placed her cereal bowl in the dishwasher when her cell chimed. She looked at the screen. A text from Becky. "Perfect timing," Honey said. The text read: "Ready to go."

Honey texted back: "OMW."

Honey dashed upstairs to get Turtle. You never knew when you might need the stuff in your backpack. And in Honey's case, she never knew when Turtle might be needed. She ran back to the kitchen, grabbed a roll of paper towels from the pantry, stuffed them into her backpack, and headed outside. She didn't get more than a few steps before she turned back around. Mrs. Wilcox was standing at the door holding Honey's rain boots and rain jacket.

"Thank you," Honey said. She went back into the kitchen, pulled on her boots, zipped her green jacket, plopped her rain hat on her head, and laughed.

"You look like a drowned daisy," Mrs. Wilcox said.

"I feel like one too."

Honey sprinted down the street, sloshing through some puddles and leaping across others until she reached Becky's house. Becky stood on the porch. She hadn't forgotten her rain gear.

"Hey," Becky called. "Let's go."

Becky and Honey headed toward the Stevenses' house.

"I hope the rain will stop soon," Becky said.

"Me too." Honey stamped mud off her boots. "I have a feeling Bart is one of those dogs that smells really bad when he gets wet."

"Yeah," Becky said. "Do you think he has a

raincoat?"

Honey shrugged and jumped a puddle. "Guess we'll find out."

They reached the Stevenses' house. No cars were in the driveway.

"Guess they left for work," Becky said.

Mrs. Stevens told Honey she would leave a key under the third flowerpot from the left on the porch. She found it lickety-split.

"Here we go," Honey said. "Our first day on the job."

Becky smiled. "I feel sort of grown up or something."

Honey pushed open the front door. Bart barked like crazy at first. "Shhhhh," Honey said. "It's just us. Honey and Becky. We're here to take you for a walk."

Bart settled down, but he did not seem

interested in going for a walk.

"That dog is no fool," Becky said. "He doesn't want to go out in the rain."

"But he has to," Honey said. She looked around. She didn't see anything that looked like a doggie raincoat for a Saint Bernard. Honey removed her floppy rain hat. "Maybe he'll wear this. It could help."

Becky laughed. Bart looked so funny in Honey's rain hat. "You might have to give him your coat too."

87

Honey clicked the leash on Bart's collar. But Bart, who was sitting half in and half out of a big armchair, would not move. Honey tugged and tugged. "Come on, Bart. You have to go out."

But no soap. The big Saint Bernard just sat there.

Becky helped tug. "Please, Bart," Becky pleaded. "You need to do your business outside. Just go and come back. Real fast."

That was when Honey spied a note on the coffee table.

Dear Sleepy Hollow Howlers,

If Bart refuses to go out in the rain, you can try to bribe him with a treat.

88

Honey grabbed the box of Sleepy Hollow Outfitters Doggy Doodles. "Come on, boy, want a treat?"

Bart moved! He wiggled his large bottom out of the chair. Honey gave him a treat. Her hand pretty much disappeared under his giant lips.

"Ewww, gross," Becky said.

"Come on, Bart," Honey said. "Let's go. I'll give you another treat."

Finally, Bart cooperated, and Honey and Becky got him outside. They didn't take a very long walk because Bart did what he had to do pretty quickly and then looked mournfully back at the house.

"He just wants to go home," Becky said.

"Then that's where we go," Honey said. "Maybe the rain will stop in time for his second walk."

Honey and Becky kept Bart on the porch for a few minutes while they dried him off with paper towels. He didn't seem to mind the attention.

"Good dog," Honey said. She took her hat back.

Bart barked.

After getting the dog settled in his chair and giving him the promised treat, Honey and Becky locked up the house, returned the key to its hiding spot, and set off down the street.

"Phew," Becky said. "That was kind of fun but also a little frustrating."

"Yeah," Honey said, "a little. But we got him out and did our job." She and Becky high-fived.

"What's next?" Becky asked.

"Let's go back to the craft room and make another sign. We need to hang one at the shelter, and I can check on Stormy."

Honey and Becky raced to Becky's house.

They were just about there when they saw Clarice Kligore, the mayor's daughter, walking down the street with two brown dogs.

"Hey, Clarice," Becky said. "I didn't know you have dogs. I thought the only hounds you have are your father's."

Clarice smirked. "Nope. I'm just walking them. It's my new business."

"Whaaaat?" Honey said.

"I saw your sign at the pet shop, and I thought it sounded like a good idea."

Becky stamped her foot. "But that's not fair, Clarice. You stole our idea."

Clarice rolled her eyes. One of her dogs sniffed around a bush. "Can't steal ideas." She smirked. "Besides, I think I'm a better dog walker. My business will be the best."

"Oh yeah," Honey said. "Let's just see about that."

"Sure, you can try," Clarice said. "But I bet I'll have the most clients by August. I'm a natural with dogs."

Honey felt like she wanted to scream. But she didn't. Instead, she just said, "Fine. You're on. The loser buys the winner a Magic Mayhem Pizza and Sleepy Hollow Banana Smoothies."

"Start saving your money," Clarice said. But all of a sudden her dogs pulled so hard that Clarice went zooming down the street like she had been shot from a rocket. Honey and Becky watched. Clarice's feet were running faster than her body. Her free arm swung like a whirligig and *pow!* Clarice tumbled into the grass.

Honey and Becky gasped. But when they saw that Clarice was okay, they laughed and then hightailed it to Becky's house.

They were soaking wet by the time they reached her front porch. Fortunately, Becky's mom was there with warm towels fresh from the dryer.

"Look at you two," she said.

"Thanks," Honey said as she dried off with the towel. "We had fun."

"Yeah," Becky said. "The dog was a little stubborn at first, but we got him outside."

"I'm proud of you both," Mrs. Young said. "Now come on inside. I have pie."

"Oh boy," Honey said. "Lemon meringue?"

93

"You bet," Mrs. Young said with a smile.

Honey thought Becky's mother made the best pie in town, especially lemon meringue. It was made with just the right amount of tartness and sweetness, which Honey figured went nicely with her personality.

After they each had enjoyed a large slice, Becky and Honey headed for the craft room. Becky made two signs, one for the shelter and one just in case they needed another one later. This time she used gold and red glitter, which gave the poster some added pizzazz.

"Great job," Honey said. "Let's go to the shelter."

Honey's phone buzzed. "Hold on," she said, "probably Mrs. Wilcox wondering where I am."

Honey tapped the screen. "Hello?"

It was not Mrs. Wilcox. It was Mrs. Tenure, their teacher. Honey looked at Becky. "It's Mrs. Tenure," she whispered.

Becky's eyes grew wide. "What did you do now?"

Honey swallowed. Why would their teacher call her? She swallowed again. "Hello, Mrs. Tenure." Honey grabbed Becky's hand for a little reassurance. An ominous rumble of thunder rolled overhead.

MRS. TENURE AND HER THREE DOGS

"Is this the Sleepy Hollow Howlers?" Mrs. Tenure asked.

Honey relaxed. There was no way Mrs. Tenure could have known she was calling Honey. They didn't put their names on the poster.

"Yes," Honey said. "We aim to paw-lease."

She smiled because she had just thought of saying that. Becky shook her head and rolled her eyes.

"Oh, that's wonderful," Mrs. Tenure said. "I would like to hire your services. I have three corgi dogs, Manny, Moe, and Jack. And I just can't possibly walk them today."

"No problem," Honey said. She held up three fingers to Becky.

"We can come to your house in a little while," Honey said.

"Fine. That's fine. But please be here before three. I have an appointment."

"Okay," Honey's heart pounded. "No problem." She clicked off the phone.

"This is weird," Honey said. "Should we go? She's our teacher."

Becky shrugged. "Why not? It's summer."

Honey dropped the phone into her backpack. She looked at Turtle's googly eyes. "What do you think?"

Turtle didn't say anything, but his eyes did wiggle around.

"I say we go," Becky said. "If she changes her mind when she finds out who we are then that's okay."

"Good idea. She's the grown-up. She can decide. And besides, we need all the clients we can get. Clarice is not going to beat the Howlers in the dog-walking game."

Honey looked through the window. The rain had stopped, and the dark clouds made way for a blue sky. "The rain stopped. Let's go to the shelter and then over to Mrs. Tenure's. She said we just need to be there before three."

Terry was behind the counter at the shelter as usual.

"Hi, Terry," Honey said. "Remember us? We

brought a sign to hang on the bulletin board."

"Oh yes," Terry said. "Go right ahead. I spoke with my supervisor, and she was happy to help."

There were some spare thumbtacks stuck in the board, so Honey had no trouble getting their sign hung up. She made sure it was front and center. She had to move a small notice about some kind of dog food recall, but it looked like it had been there for a long time.

Honey went back to Terry, who was now talking with another person. Honey and Becky waited and waited until, finally, Isabela came out from the back.

"Isabela," Honey said. "How's Stormy?"

"Hi," Isabela said. "She's doing great. Want to visit?"

"I sure do," Honey said.

Honey and Becky followed Isabela to the isolation wing. Honey looked through the door.

Stormy was busy chewing a rag doll, and now she was wearing a red-and-white bandana.

"Cool bandana," Becky said.

"Yeah," Honey agreed. "She looks so happy."

"She is," Isabela said. "I wish I could adopt her."

"I know the feeling," Honey said. "But we already have a dog."

99

"Me too," Becky said. "My dad's allergic."

Terry appeared with the man she was talking to. "Could this be your dog?"

Honey's heart sped up. Maybe it was. Maybe Stormy would be going home.

The tall man looked through the window. He shook his head. "No, that's not her."

Honey felt sad when the man turned away. He looked sad also.

"Keep looking," Isabela said. "Your dog will come back."

"I hope so," the man said. "I really miss her."

Terry led the man out of the isolation wing. "I'm glad she seems so happy," Becky said. "But it still must be hard being caged up so much."

"It is," Isabela said. "But I was just about to bring her out for her walk."

"Oh," Honey said. "Becky and I have to go see another client about her dogs. She has three corgis."

"Three?" Becky said. "Is that what you were trying to tell me? How can we walk three dogs at once?"

"That's easy," Isabela said. "Don't worry, you'll figure it out. Just keep a firm hold on the leash. Don't let go, and make sure the dogs know you're the boss."

"Good advice." Honey tapped on the glass

Mrs. Tenure's house. This was going to be weird.

"I guess it's okay," Honey said.

"Why not?" Becky asked as they turned down Skeleton Lane. "We're not doing anything wrong."

"Guess we'll find out."

Mrs. Tenure lived in a small house with a small porch. A large, spreading oak stood like a sentinel in front of the house. She also had rose bushes that were blooming and many lawn ornaments—gnomes and bunnies as well as a few Sleepy Hollow-like statues, including a ghost and a skeleton.

Honey knocked on the door. The three corgis yipped and yapped like mad until Mrs. Tenure opened the door.

"Honey," Mrs. Tenure said. "What are you doing here?"

"We're the Sleepy Hollow Howlers." Then

to get Stormy's attention. "She's so cute."

"I need to walk the dogs now," Isabela said. And when she did, Honey got a brilliant idea. She looked at Becky, "Are you thinking what I'm thinking?"

Becky nodded.

"Isabela," Honey said. "How would you like to come help us walk Bart later? If you can, of course."

Isabela smiled widely. "Maybe. What time?"

"Three o'clock. Becky and I will come get you here, and we can walk over to his house together. Will you be finished volunteering here by then?"

"That's perfect," Isabela said. "I'm done at two thirty today."

"Great," Honey said. "We'll be back."

First, Honey and Becky had to go over to

she smiled and raised her eyebrows. "Sorry, we didn't put our names on the posters."

Mrs. Tenure stepped out onto the porch. "Oh, that's okay."

"Oh no," Becky said, "What happened?" She pointed to the bright pink cast on Mrs. Tenure's left leg.

"That's why I can't walk the dogs," she said. "I slipped down the stairs and cracked my ankle."

103

"I'm so sorry, Mrs. Tenure," Becky said.

"We'll be glad to help with the dogs and anything else you need," Honey said. "We can go to the store if you need us to."

"Oh, that would be grand," Mrs. Tenure said. "I'll pay you of course."

That was when Honey felt the weight of Turtle on her back. "Oh no," Honey said. "You can pay us for the dog walking because that's our business. But the other errands are free of charge."

"We just want to help," Becky said.

"Well, that's very kind of you," Mrs. Tenure said. "Now come in and meet the boys. They might yip a little, but they're very sweet."

Honey laughed when she saw the dogs. "Gee, even if you stood all three of those guys on top of each other, they're still smaller than the Saint Bernard we walked this morning."

Mrs. Tenure laughed. "Oh, I know him. His owners walked him past here a few days ago. Nice people. New to town. We talked for a while."

Manny, Moe, and Jack yipped and sniffed around Becky's feet. Manny jumped into Honey's lap the second she sat on the sofa.

"Oh, look, they like you," Mrs. Tenure said. "You can get started right away. And boy, am I glad Miss Muffet called to let me know about your service. Poor little pooches haven't had a good walk in a week."

"Sleepy Hollow Howlers to the rescue," Honey said.

But Becky was not quite as enthusiastic from what Honey could tell. At the moment, one of the dogs was still sniffing her ankles while another sat in her lap.

"Are you okay, Becky?" Mrs. Tenure asked.

"Y-y-yes, I think so," Becky said. "But three dogs at once."

"Oh, they're such good walkers," Mrs. Tenure said. "You'll see."

Honey looked around Mrs. Tenure's house. It was not exactly how she might have pictured it—not that she ever had. Mrs. Tenure had a lot of pictures. Mostly family, Honey figured, but also some pretty wild abstract paintings and a small statue of a weird-looking dog. Mrs. Tenure must have noticed Honey looking at it.

"That's pre-Columbian art," Mrs. Tenure said. "It's quite old."

"It's nice," Honey said, even though she had never seen a dog like that before. It had a fat body and little ears. Kind of like a Chihuahua except its mouth was open exposing lots of sharp, tiny teeth.

Honey and Becky attached the leashes to the dogs and set out on their walk. Mrs. Tenure was right. The dogs were very happy to be out. They ran out ahead of them at first, and Honey and Becky had to pull them back.

"Whoaaaa," Becky said. "They're like little ponies."

"They're stronger than I thought," Honey said, "for having such little legs."

Honey had two dogs. One in each hand. She was pretty sure they were Manny and Moe. Moe was on her right. She thought she had them settled when Moe caught sight of a squirrel. He yipped once and then took off like a rocket. Honey couldn't hold on, and he pulled the leash out of her hand.

"Oh no," Honey hollered. She ran after him. But he was so quick. He dashed through yards and around trees trying to catch the squirrel. Honey gave Becky Manny's leash. "Stay here while I chase Moe."

Honey ran. "Moe," she called. "Stop doggy.

107

Stop." But Moe kept running until he somehow got his leash hooked on a lawn chair. He stopped for a second, and Honey was just about to grab the leash when he took off again. This time dragging the lawn chair with him. He bolted right over a scarecrow and into a fake spider web on someone's lawn.

"This is a disaster," Honey called. "Stop Moe. Please STOP!"

108   Then, thankfully, Titus Kligore, Mayor Kligore's son, showed up.

"Stop that dog," Honey hollered.

Titus took a few steps and scooped the little dog up in his arms and untangled the leash from the chair. "Gotcha," he said.

Honey stopped running. "Phew, thank you, Titus."

"When did you get a little dog?" Titus asked.

Honey shook her head and explained to

Titus about her new business.

"Oh, okay," Titus said. "My sister's doing that too. You know you don't have a chance of getting more clients than my sister."

Honey took Moe from Titus. "No way, Titus. And you can tell Clarice I said so."

Titus just lifted his chin toward her, "Sure you will." He walked on. Stopped and turned around. "How can you get more clients when you can't even control that tiny thing?"

Honey covered Moe's ears. "He's not a thing."

Titus shook his head and smirked the same way Clarice always smirked. It was definitely genetic.

Becky caught up with Honey. "Are you okay?"

"Yeah," Honey said. "But that chair is destroyed." Moe squirmed in her arms, so she set him down. He was immediately greeted by

his two brothers.

"Guess we'll have to pay for it," Becky said.

"Guess so. And we just got started in business. We're losing our profits already."

"Come on," Becky said. "Let's bring the chair back."

"And the dogs," Honey said.

110

Honey held all three leashes while Becky carried the broken lawn chair.

Manny, Moe, and Jack were much better behaved.

Becky and Honey went to the house where Moe had latched onto the chair. An older gentleman answered Honey's knock on the door. Honey explained the whole thing. For a moment, the man just looked at her. Then he looked at the dogs. Then he looked back at Honey.

"We'd like to pay for the chair," Honey said. "But we can't until we get paid more."

And that was when the man started to laugh. "I saw the whole thing," he said through his laughter. "It was quite a show. I didn't think you'd ever catch that dog. Good thing that boy came along when he did."

Honey didn't quite know what to say.

"Look," the man said. "It was an old chair. Don't worry about it. I needed a good laugh today. No charge."

111

"Thank you," Honey said.

But as she and Becky made their way back to Mrs. Tenure's, Honey didn't feel so well. Her stomach had a knot the size of a basketball.

"Maybe this is too hard," she told Becky.

Becky let out a big sigh. "Maybe it is."

112

A CRUCIAL BUSINESS DECISION

Manny, Moe, and Jack were happy to get home. Honey told Mrs. Tenure what happened.

"I tried to hang on to him, but for a little dog, he sure is strong."

Mrs. Tenure laughed a little, but then she grew more serious. "It's not all your fault, Honey. Moe can be a bit of a rascal. He's gotten away from me a few times."

"Thank you for saying that," Honey said.

"But the rest of the walk went great," Becky added.

"I'm glad to hear it," Mrs. Tenure said. "Becky, will you hand me my purse? It's just over there on the dining room table."

"Oh, it's okay," Honey. "You don't have to pay us. Your dog got away. And that chair got broken."

Becky handed Mrs. Tenure her bag. She opened it and removed a colorful wallet. "Nonsense, you performed a service. Things happen all the time, and people still collect their fee."

Honey took a breath and sighed. "Thank you."

There were still a few hours before they had to go to the Stevenses' house and walk Bart.

Who would have thought that three little dogs would be more trouble than one huge Saint Bernard?

"Let's go to my house," Honey said. "We can hang out there until it's time to get Isabela."

"Okay," Becky said. She hopped across a leftover puddle. "I like her."

"Me too," Honey said. "But I also feel sad for her. She lives in a foster home."

Becky shrugged. "But she seems really happy."

"She is, I think. I just think she would really like a forever home."

Mrs. Wilcox was playing with Harvest in the front yard while Half Moon lazed on the porch.

"Honey," Harvest called.

"Hey there, little bro," Honey said. "How's it

going?"

Mrs. Wilcox clambered to her feet. "Honey," she said. "How was the first day on the job?"

"Okay, I guess," Honey said.

Mrs. Wilcox pushed a few stray gray hairs off her face and adjusted her glasses. "Just okay?"

Honey tousled Harvest's hair. "Yeah, just okay. It started out good. We walked a giant Saint Bernard, but then we walked three corgis and . . ."

"We had a little incident," Becky said. "One of the dogs got away from Honey and went on a rampage."

"A rampage?" Mrs. Wilcox said. Her eyes grew wide. "Oh dear."

"Not exactly a rampage," Honey said. "But he ran all around, through people's yards, and even got his leash hooked on a lawn chair and dragged it all over."

Mrs. Wilcox put her hand over her mouth like she was hiding a laugh. "But you got him back, I imagine."

Honey nodded. "And Mrs. Tenure was really nice about it. But still—"

"Oh, I wouldn't feel too bad about it if I were you," Mrs. Wilcox said. "Dogs are known to do that sort of thing."

Honey played peek-a-boo with Harvest who was giggling wildly. "I guess it made me wonder if I can really do the job."

"Certainly you can, Honey Moon," Mrs. Wilcox said. "The Honey Moon I know can do anything she sets her mind to."

Honey smiled. "Thanks, Mrs. Wilcox." But deep inside, Honey still had her doubts. "What if Moe had run away for good?"

"Then you would have dealt with it. Life throws curve balls all the time. Have to know how to swing at them."

Honey and Becky started up the porch steps. Half Moon still snored away.

"There's fresh chicken salad in the fridge," Mrs. Wilcox said. "You girls are probably hungry."

"Sounds good," Becky said. "I could go for a sandwich."

Before Honey opened the refrigerator, her eye caught the picture of Anisha. She let out a sigh when she remembered one of the reasons she wanted to walk dogs—to purchase a proper homework desk for Anisha.

She grabbed the container of chicken salad, set it on the kitchen table, and said to Becky, "I can't quit. Anisha needs me. And I always go where I am needed. I don't give up."

"Of course you can do this," Becky said as she placed two slices of bread on a paper towel. "Today was just our first day. We will definitely learn as we go."

"And," Honey said as she slathered chicken

118

salad on bread, "if Isabela joins the team then we'll have three people to walk the corgis. She's a professional."

Honey felt better as she finished building her sandwich.

After lunch, Honey and Becky went to Honey's room to wait until it was time to pick up Isabela. Summer had a way of being full of fun and things to do and plenty of times of doing nothing and feeling bored. And for a little while anyway, Honey and Becky were feeling pretty bored. Until Harry burst into her room. Usually Honey was the one who burst into Harry's room.

119

"Hey, what are you doing?" Honey asked. "You can't just barge in like a rhino."

"I was wondering how your dog-walking biz was going," Harry said. "I heard from Bailey that you were seen racing through yards and jumping fences chasing someone's dog." He laughed.

Honey shook her head. "How did your nerdy friend know?"

"Bailey lives on the same street as Mrs. Tenure. He saw you." Harry laughed some more. "He said it was quite a sight. I wish I was there. But I was still over at Hao's house."

"Don't give her a hard time," Becky said. "We were walking three dogs at once. It was pretty crazy, especially when Moe got his leash caught around the lawn chair and started dragging it all over." Becky put her hand over her mouth. "I'm sorry. It was kind of funny."

Honey thought she might get a little angry, but then she couldn't help it, and she started to laugh. "You should have seen him. His little legs were running sixty miles an hour."

"Well, he couldn't help it," Becky said. "Mrs. Tenure said they hadn't been out for a good walk in a long time."

Honey picked up Turtle and hugged him to her chest. "I'm just glad I caught up with him.

And I'm also glad the man who owned the lawn chair didn't get angry." Then she looked up at Harry. She noticed his DO NO EVIL T-shirt. It was the shirt the Good Mischief Team wore when they were doing their good deeds. She got a brilliant idea.

"Becky," she said. "You know what we need?"

"What?"

"T-shirts. We need Sleepy Hollow Howlers T-shirts. It will make us look official and like we are a real business."

"Good idea," Becky said.

"Sure is." Harry leaned against the bedroom door. "I bet Dad will be happy to make them for you."

Honey's dad had a small screen-printing press in the garage. He printed Harry's T-shirts all the time.

122

"And I can design it," Becky said. "We'll need a logo. Maybe the dog I drew on our posters."

"Perfect," Honey said.

Honey and Becky high-fived. "Sleepy Hollow Howlers!"

Becky would get to work on the design right away, but Honey would have to wait until her father got home from work to ask him. But she was certain he would say yes.

The Spooktacular Barkathon

Becky and Honey hurried over to the shelter to pick up Isabela. It certainly wouldn't take all three of them to walk Bart. But Honey was secretly glad she had back up. You just never knew with dogs.

Honey saw a sign in front of the shelter.

THIS SATURDAY

SLEEPY HOLLOW ANIMAL SHELTER

MAYOR MAXIMUS KLIGORE'S

Spooktacular
BARKATHON

All dogs half price

"Hey, look at that," Becky said. "A barkathon."

"That's great," Honey said. "I'm sure Stormy will get a home now."

Honey was just about to push open the shelter door when she saw Isabela through the glass. She waved.

Isabela pushed open the door. Hey, I'm ready to go."

"Great," Honey said.

"Guess what?" Becky said as the girls set off down the street.

"What," Isabela asked.

"We are going to have Sleepy Hollow Howlers T-shirts."

"That's a great idea," Isabela said.

Honey thought it would be a good idea to cut through the town green on their way to the Stevenses' house.

"Ugh," Isabela said. "What is with the Headless Horseman? I mean it was a great story and all, but everyone knows the real Headless Horseman story took place in New York."

Honey laughed. "That's what started the whole thing. People were coming here in search of the Horseman and getting upset when they discovered they were in the wrong state."

"Can you imagine?" Becky said.

Isabela laughed.

"So, Mayor Kligore managed to turn the

whole town into Spooky Town and celebrate old horseface." Honey hiked Turtle higher onto her shoulders. Old horseface never seemed quite so scary with Turtle on her back.

"I get it," Isabela said. "I guess it makes sense."

Honey picked up a twig and tossed it toward the statue. "Just don't let the mayor fool you. He's up to no good. My brother knows all about him."

"What do you mean?"

Honey felt Turtle on her back. "My brother is convinced that Mayor Kligore and his whole icky company, the We Drive By Night Company, is really up to evil things. Harry is out to stop them."

Isabela stopped walking and grabbed Honey's arm. "Seriously? Aren't you scared?"

Turtle grew heavier. Honey smiled. "I'm not afraid of the dark. And you shouldn't be

either."

"That's right," Becky said. "Harry Moon has got it all under control. Harry is fighting the evil with good. That's the Good Mischief Team's motto. DO NO EVIL."

The trio rounded the corner.

"Good to know," Isabela said. "I get scared kind of easily—not of dogs or lightning but that dark magic kind of stuff bugs me."

"Me too," Honey said. "That's why I try and help Harry whenever I can."

"Look," Becky said. "Bart's already in his yard."

"Uh oh," Honey said. They picked up their pace. "How did he get out?"

Honey started to run toward the Stevenses' house. She did not need two disasters in one day.

When Honey reached the yard's gate, Bart

bounded toward her. He leaped up on the gate. He barked once.

Honey patted his head. "Hey, Bart. How'd you get out?"

Becky reached up and patted him. "Yeah. Did you leave the door open, Honey?"

"No," Honey said. "I remember locking it and replacing the key under the flower pot." But then she got a terrible, sinking feeling in the pit of her stomach. "Clarice! Maybe she let him out."

"How could she do that?" Becky asked.

Honey looked around the yard. "Maybe she saw us put the key under the flowerpot. Maybe she's out to torpedo us."

Becky laughed a little. "I seriously doubt that."

"He's incredible," Isabela said. "Gorgeous dog. I always wanted a Saint Bernard."

That was when the front door opened, and Mrs. Stevens stepped onto the porch.

Relief washed over Honey. "Oh, good, she's home."

"Here, Bart," Mrs. Stevens called. "Come on."

Bart lumbered back to the porch. Honey pushed open the gate. "Hi, Mrs. Stevens, we're here for Bart's walk. That is if you still need us."

"Sure do," she said. "I have his leash right here."

Honey introduced Isabela to Mrs. Stevens. "This is Isabela Bonito; she'll be walking with us. She works at the animal shelter."

"Oh, really," Mrs. Stevens said.

"I volunteer," Isabela replied. "Your dog is the most beautiful dog I have ever seen."

Mrs. Stevens smiled widely. "Thank you. He's quite a handful, though."

Isabela hugged the big dog around the neck. "Would it be okay if I took the leash first?"

"Sure," Honey said.

"Wow," Mrs. Stevens said. "He really seems to like you, Isabela."

Isabela smiled. "I have a way with dogs." She attached the leash to Bart's collar and off the Howlers went with Bart leading the way.

But then, Isabela did something that Honey thought was kind of magical. She pulled the leash slightly and stopped walking. Bart tried to pull her along, but she stood her ground, and the big guy stopped also.

"Over here, Bart," she said. "Walk next to me."

Bart let out a deep woof. Isabela pulled the leash again, and Bart did exactly what Isabela asked. She reached into her pocket and pulled out a skull-shaped doggie treat. Bart chomped it with glee. Then she set off with Bart keeping almost perfect stride with her.

"You're like a dog whisperer," Honey said. "That's amazing."

"It just takes a firm but gentle hand. You don't want the dog thinking he's the alpha in the pack. And it's always wise to carry treats in your pocket."

Honey and Becky looked at each other. "Makes sense," Honey said. "But not always that easy."

131

The Howlers finished their walk with Bart and headed back to the Stevenses' house. Bart, who was pretty well-behaved for most of the walk, yanked the leash away from Isabela and darted through the gate and up the porch steps like a rocket.

Isabela laughed. "Sometimes, the dog is stronger."

Mrs. Stevens opened the door and invited them inside. "Come in. I made lemonade, and I think I might have a nice pound cake also."

"Thank you," Honey said.

"Gee, thanks," Becky said as they followed Mrs. Stevens inside.

Bart went right for his water bowl.

"He seems so happy," Mrs. Stevens said.

132

"Isabela is a natural," Honey said. "She was so good with him. He just walked beside her like she was the queen."

"Alpha," Isabela said.

"Sort of the same thing." Becky sat at the kitchen table.

Mrs. Stevens poured lemonade into three tumblers.

Isabela finished hers quickly.

"How about a slice of cake?" Mrs. Stevens asked.

No, thank you," Isabela said. "My foster mother is probably wondering where I am. I better get going."

Mrs. Stevens looked at Isabela. "Oh, all right, Isabela. I hope I see you again."

"You will," Honey said. "She's a member of the Howlers now."

Isabela set her glass on the counter. "I'll see

you tomorrow, right?"

"Right," Honey said.

"And I can help earlier tomorrow. I have the day off."

"Great," Honey said when she pulled her glass from her lips. "We have three corgis first thing in the morning. Sure can use your help. I'll text you the time."

"Terrific," Isabela said. "See you tomorrow." She patted Bart's head. "See you, big guy."

Bart lifted his sloppy face toward her like he was about to give her a dog kiss. But Isabela turned away just in time to miss Bart's slobber.

Mrs. Stevens grabbed some paper towels and wiped Bart's face. "He's like a toddler. A giant toddler."

Honey walked Isabela to the front door. "Thanks a lot. You are amazing with dogs."

"Thanks," Isabela said looking at her feet.

"By the way," Honey asked. "How's Stormy doing?"

"She's doing great. She'll be out of isolation tomorrow. Just in time for the Barkathon. I'm sure someone will adopt her. She's a pretty sweet dog."

"Oh, right, the Barkathon," Honey said.

135

"You should come—even if you're not in the market for a dog. Terry said it's a blast."

"Okay," Honey said. "I'd love to see Stormy get adopted." Then she looked into Isabela's dark eyes. "How come you like the dogs so much?"

Isabela looked away from Honey. "I guess I know what it's like to feel all alone."

Honey gave Isabela a hug. "Well, you have us now."

Honey watched Isabela take off down the street. When she turned back, she saw Mrs. Stevens standing there.

"What did Isabela mean when she said she knows what it's like to be alone?"

"Oh, I think she just meant that she understands because of being a foster kid. The home she's in now is her third. She says it's a good place, just not a *real* place."

Mrs. Stevens looked past Honey for a moment. "Yeah, I get that." Then she looked at Honey. "Let me get you paid, and we'll see you tomorrow?"

"You bet," Honey said. "Two times tomorrow again?"

Mrs. Stevens snagged a backpack from a hook near the front door. Honey smiled when she saw the Sleepy Hollow Outfitter's logo on the bag.

After she had paid the bill, Mrs. Stevens

asked Honey, "You say Isabela volunteers at the shelter?"

"That's right," Becky said. "You should see her with the dogs."

"Yeah," Honey said. "It's kind of magical."

"Uhm," was all Mrs. Stevens said before Honey and Becky headed out the door.

138

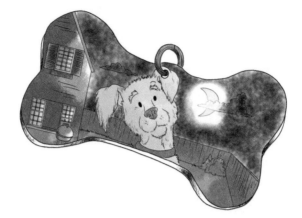

Isabela Drops Out

On the way home, Honey was lost in thought, so much so that she smacked right into a telephone pole. "Where did that come from?" she said after she regained her balance.

"It's always been there," Becky said. "You just walked right into it."

Honey rubbed her head. "You sure?"

"What's wrong with you?" Becky asked.

Nothing. I was just thinking that Isabela is sad. She wants a real home."

Becky plucked a dandelion from the ground. "I know. But what can we do? I'm sure there's someone, somewhere working on that for her."

"Maybe," Honey said. "Or maybe she's been forgotten."

For the rest of the day, Honey had a hard time getting Isabela off her mind. She tried to think about what it might be like to not have a mom or dad or a place to call home forever, but she couldn't—not really.

When she arrived home and saw her mom and Mrs. Wilcox talking in the kitchen, she almost started to cry. Her mom must have noticed something because she said, "Honey, are you okay?"

Honey sat at the kitchen table and fiddled with the salt shaker. "Yeah, I was just thinking

how good it is that I have you and Dad and Harvest and even Harry and Half Moon and Mrs. Wilcox—forever."

Honey's mom said goodbye to Mrs. Wilcox who patted Honey on the shoulder. "I'm glad you are in my life too, Honey."

"Thanks," Honey said.

After she had walked Mrs. Wilcox to her car, Honey's mom sat at the table. "Did something trigger this today?" she asked.

"I think it's Isabela, my new friend from the shelter."

Honey's mom nodded. "Oh right, she's a foster kid."

"Right, and I know she wants a forever home, a real home, so much. I wish I could do something."

Mary Moon patted Honey's hand. "Oh, sweetie," she said. "You can't, not really. I'm sure there is an agency working on it. Helping to get Stormy a forever home is way different."

"I know. But I also know I met Isabela for a reason. You know, like Harry is always talking about, it's a destiny thing."

Mary Moon took a deep breath and sighed it away. "Possibly, but don't get too hung up on it. Now, how about peeling some potatoes for dinner?"

"You gonna mash them?"

"Yep, just for you."

After supper that day, Honey sat in her room. Another rainstorm had moved in. It was not as bad as the night she found Stormy, but there was still some booms of thunder and crackles of lightning.

Honey sat on her bed reading one of her favorite books—*The Dolphins*. She was reading number nine in the series. Becky was already up to number twelve. She turned the page to chapter seven when her eye caught sight of Turtle. Her backpack was lying in a crumple on the floor where she had tossed it. She could see Turtle's googly eyes. There was just something about the neon-green backpack that eased Honey's fears, calmed her worries, and, most of the time, just made her feel secure.

"What can I do, Turtle?"

It wasn't long before a thought popped into her head, as it so often did when she talked to Turtle. "You are already doing it," Turtle said.

143

Before she could say anything further to Turtle, a loud thunderclap boomed overhead accompanied by a crackle of lightning that lit up her room. Seconds later, Harvest burst through the door.

"Honey," he cried. "I'm scared."

Honey helped Harvest onto her bed. "Awww, it's just rain and thunder and lightning. But I know it can be scary."

Harvest's bottom lip quivered. Honey pulled him close for a hug. "You can stay here until it passes."

But the rain didn't end until morning, and Honey was awakened by her mom.

"Harvest," she exclaimed. "Have you been here all night?"

Honey sat up. "Yes, Mom, he was scared of the storm."

Harvest giggled and climbed off the bed.

"Come on," Mary Moon said. "Let's get you some breakfast."

"Cheerios," Harvest yelled and dashed out the door.

Honey's mom stood at the doorway. "Thanks for looking out for Harvest."

"Sure thing," Honey said. "He's my brother."

144

Honey's mom smiled. "Get dressed and come down for breakfast. Are you walking dogs today?"

"We sure are," Honey said. "A Saint Bernard and three corgis. I am hoping to get some more calls."

"You will," Mary Moon said. "I'm sure word of mouth will start spreading soon. That's how Harry's Good Mischief Team got so busy. Now come down quickly, I have a surprise for you."

"A surprise? What is it?"

"If I tell you it won't be a surprise anymore. Now hurry up."

Honey took a quick shower and dressed. She chose her yellow shorts, a black-and-white, striped shirt, and blue ankle socks with flamingos on them. She looked at her reflection in the mirror. "Eclectic."

"There you are," Honey's mom said when Honey walked into the kitchen. "Cheerios or

Krispies?"

"Cheerios," Harvest called. "Cheerios."

"All right, all right, I'll have Cheerios. But what I really want is my surprise."

"Patience," Mary Moon said. "Eat your breakfast first, and drink all the orange juice. It's good for you."

While Honey was eating, her mother disappeared into the laundry room. *Ugh*, Honey thought, *my surprise is extra laundry.* But, instead, her mom came back with a small stack of neatly folded pink T-shirts.

"Here you go," Mary Moon said. "Your father finished them last night."

Honey felt her eyes grow big. "You mean my Sleepy Hollow Howlers T-shirts?" She grabbed one of the shirts and held it up. "Oh, Mom. It's spectacular. I love it. Now we are a real business."

"That's right," Mary Moon said.

The shirt read Sleepy Hollow Howlers across the front and on the back was the silhouette image of a dog howling at a full moon.

"They're terrific, Mom," Honey said. "Where's Dad?"

"He left for the office. But he was so happy to make them for you. He's very proud of you, Honey Moon."

"Thanks, Mom."

"Now go put one on. You look like a bumble bee in that outfit you're wearing."

"Of course, I do," Honey said. "I'm a honey bee."

Honey grabbed the shirt and dashed upstairs to change. She pulled the new T-shirt on and looked in the mirror.

The shirt not only looked great but it also made Honey feel more like a professional, more like the Howlers were a real company. "Now maybe word of mouth will spread faster when people see our shirts."

Honey grabbed Turtle and headed downstairs.

"It looks great," her mom said. "Professional."

"I know. I just love them. I can't wait to give one to Becky and Isabela. They're gonna go wild."

"Well, I hope not too wild," Mary Moon said.

Honey pushed the other shirts into her backpack and slung it over her shoulder. "See you later, Mom."

On the way to Becky's, Honey texted Isabela. "Mt us at Horseman."

But it wasn't until she got to Becky's house that Isabela texted her back. "Sorry. Can't go."

Honey stared at the text. "I don't get it."

She looked up and saw Becky standing on the porch. "Don't get what?"

"Isabela. She says she can't make it today."

Becky looked at the text. "That's odd. She was so excited yesterday."

"Speaking of excited," Honey said. "Did you notice my T-shirt?"

Becky took a step back. "It's outstanding.

Your dad works fast."

Honey reached into her backpack. "Yep. You know him; he loves to make T-shirts."

Becky turned her shirt around. "And look. He used my drawing. It looks great."

"Go change, Honey said.

"Be back in a flash." Becky bolted into her house.

"Do you think we should go see what's up with Isabela?" Becky asked after she changed her shirt.

"You mean go to her house?" Honey asked as they started down the walkway.

Becky shrugged. "Why not? Maybe she's sick or something."

"Nah, she would have said she was sick."

When they turned onto Broom Stick Drive,

Honey stopped. "Hey, I don't even know where she lives."

"I do," Becky said. "She told me yesterday. She actually lives close to the Stevenses. Like right down the street in that old house. The yellow one with the green shutters."

Honey and Becky walked on. "Should we go?" Becky asked.

Turtle grew a little heavier. "I'm not sure. Let me text her again."

151

Honey's thumbs flew over the keys. "Are you okay? Can we come ovr?"

They waited. A few seconds later, Honey's phone chimed.

"Sry. Jst can't."

Honey shook her head. "Well, that settles it. We're going."

"Are you sure?" Becky asked.

"Yes," Honey said. "She's not sick. Something is wrong, and I think she needs us. And like I always say, I go where I am needed."

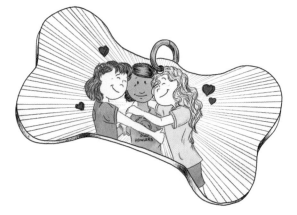

MEETING
MISS MAPLELEAF

The house where Isabela lived was the second biggest house in Sleepy Hollow. It sat on a large lot that bordered Folly Farm, where Mayor Kligore lived in the biggest house—a huge mansion with lots of rooms and, Honey heard, six bathrooms. Honey thought the Kligore mansion was creepy.

But Isabela's house was not at all scary.

"It reminds me of the gingerbread dollhouse my mom and I made," Becky said.

"Yeah," Honey said. "That's what they call all that fancy woodwork around the roof and porch. Gingerbread."

Becky smiled. "I like it. But, what do we do now? Just stand here and wait for her to come out?"

"No, that would be silly. And besides, we'll be late for Mrs. Tenure's corgis."

"Right," Becky said. "So you just gonna ring the bell?"

"Guess so," Honey said. "I can be brave."

Honey and Becky approached the front door. It was a big door with lots of worm holes and swirls of wood. It had a large lion head knocker right in the center.

Honey used it, and a loud *clang* reverberated around them.

"I take it back," Honey said. "It is a little scary."

The door opened, and there stood a small, plump woman with rosy cheeks and gray hair pulled back in a bun. She wore a blue-and-white flowered dress and a yellow apron with what looked like berry stains. Honey caught the aroma of sugar and butter like the woman had been baking.

"Can I help you?" the woman asked.

"Yes," Honey said. "We were looking for Isabela."

"Oh, Isabela," the woman said. "You must be Honey and Becky. She told me about you last night. I'm Miss Mapleleaf."

"Pleased to meet you," Honey said remembering her manners. "Isabela was supposed to walk dogs with us this morning. We got worried when she canceled."

"Canceled?" Miss Mapleleaf said. "Uhm. Let me check on her. Wait right here."

"She seems nice," Becky said.

"Really nice," Honey said looking around. "Look at all those flower pots."

"Wow," Becky said. "She must really like flowers."

A few minutes later, Miss Mapleleaf reappeared at the door. "I'm sorry, girls," she said. "But Isabela isn't feeling well this morning. She said to go on without her."

"Oh, okay, but . . . well, look," Honey said, "give her this." She unzipped Turtle and gave the woman a T-shirt.

"How sweet," Miss Mapleleaf said. "It's very kind of you."

"Thanks," Honey said.

156

"Yeah, thanks," Becky said. And they headed down the walk.

But just as they reached the street, they heard Isabela.

Honey spun around. Isabela was standing on the porch waving the T-shirt. "Wait for me," she called.

"Okay," Honey said.

"Wow," Becky said. "She changed her mind fast."

"I am so glad," Honey said. "I knew she wasn't sick. I think she gets sad sometimes."

"Yeah, that must be it. Maybe the T-shirt cheered her up."

"Probably. Maybe it made her feel like she belonged in some way."

Isabela ran down the path. "Sorry. I love this T-shirt. Thanks."

"Okay," Honey said. "First we have Mrs. Tenure's dogs."

"Yeah," Becky said. "She has three of them."

"No problem." Isabela turned back and waved to Miss Mapleleaf. "And are we walking Bart too?"

"Yep," Honey said. We have him two times a day."

158

"Cool," Isabela said. "Let's go."

Mrs. Tenure was waiting on the porch. She was standing kind of awkwardly on her crutches. The dogs were yipping and yapping.

"I guess they heard us," Becky said as she pushed open the gate.

"Good morning, girls," Mrs. Tenure said. "The boys are ready for their walk."

"Good morning," Honey replied. "This is Isabela. She's new."

"Oh, Isabela," Mrs. Tenure said. "Are you the girl who moved in with Miss Mapleleaf?"

"Yes," Isabela said. She looked at the ground like she did yesterday.

Honey felt her eyebrows rise. "How do you know?"

"Well, I know because she'll be joining our class."

159

"Oh," Honey said. "That's right, Isabela. Mrs. Tenure is our teacher."

Isabela managed a small smile. But she didn't say anything.

"Well," Mrs. Tenure said. "I guess you can get the doggies on their leashes."

"And hopefully Moe won't run away again," Honey said with a laugh.

"Hopefully," Mrs. Tenure said.

Once again, Isabela's dog whisperer talents did not fail to impress. Manny walked with Isabela with ease. For the whole walk, Manny never tried to pull away. Moe and Jack were not so well-behaved, but they didn't cause any trouble. Except a little when a slinky, gray cat sauntered past them. Moe barked like mad, but Honey held on tight.

"How come you're so good with dogs?" Becky asked.

Isabela shrugged. "I don't know. It just happened. I love them, and they know it."

When they arrived back at Mrs. Tenure's with no reports of misbehaving or on-the-loose dogs this time, Honey felt quite proud of the Sleepy Hollow Howlers.

"It went great today," she said.

"That's fine," Mrs. Tenure said. "They do look happy. Would you like to come in for iced tea? It's getting warm."

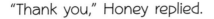
"Thank you," Honey replied.

"Yes, thank you," said Isabela and Becky.

Mrs. Tenure asked Isabela a couple of questions that Honey thought were inappropriate, but coming from an adult and a teacher, she supposed it was okay.

"So how are you getting along with Miss Mapleleaf?"

Isabela smiled. "I like her just fine. She's very kind, and she makes the best butter cookies I've ever eaten."

"Yes," Mrs. Tenure said. "They are legendary here in Sleepy Hollow."

"Oh, yeah," Becky said. "I remember her now. She was at the Christmas bazaar last year. Those cookies really are amazing."

"But I guess it can still be lonely," Mrs. Tenure said.

"Sometimes," Isabela replied. "Sometimes, I really wish I could stop moving."

Mrs. Tenure's eyes twinkled. Honey knew that twinkle. She saw it every time Mrs. Tenure had a surprise in class. It was usually a pop quiz, but a couple of times it also meant a pizza party. But she seriously doubted Mrs. Tenure was planning a pizza party now.

That afternoon, the Sleepy Hollow Howlers met at the Stevenses' house.

"Listen to that dog bark," Isabela said. "He knows we're here."

"How can he?" Becky asked. "We're standing outside. He can't see through walls."

"Dogs are very smart, and they have great senses. Believe me, he knows."

Honey got the key from under the flower pot and opened the front door. Bart practically bounded down the steps. He was so excited to see them. And he was so excited for his walk.

"Quick," Honey said. "Grab his leash."

Becky ran inside the house and found the leash hanging near the door.

"And don't forget the poop bags," Honey called.

Isabela hooked the leash onto Bart's collar. Then she looked into the big dog's eyes and patted his head. "What a good boy. We're gonna take a nice walk now. But remember your manners."

163

Bart let out a loud woof.

As they walked, Honey took the opportunity to ask Isabela some more questions. She figured that Mrs. Tenure had kind of broken the ice.

"Miss Mapleleaf's house is really huge," Honey said.

Isabela, who had control of Bart, said. "Yeah, it's okay. But big isn't always best. I like the Stevenses' house. It's cute and cozy."

"So you prefer cute and cozy," Honey said. Honey's wheels were turning. "And you really like Bart. So you like cute and cozy houses with big dogs in them."

"I guess so," Isabela said. "But Miss Mapleleaf is really nice, don't get me wrong. It's the best house I've lived in since my parents died in a car crash a few years back."

Honey swallowed. "I didn't want to ask."

"It was a drunk driver," Isabela said. "I was only five. And since my parents moved here from Ecuador, there was no other family in America. I guess that's why I feel alone so much."

Isabela pushed some stray hairs behind her ears. A small, crooked smile inched across her face, but Honey thought her eyes looked sad and far away. Maybe all the way to Ecuador.

"Ecuador is a long way away," Honey said. "Do you remember it?" She stopped walking and sat cross-legged on the grass. So did Becky and Isabela. Bart plopped down beside Isabela and rested his big head on her knee.

"Not too much," Isabela said as she sat down. "It was okay, I guess. We didn't have much money. I know that is why my parents moved here—I'm pretty sure they wanted me to have a better life."

165

Honey patted Isabela's shoulder. "Destiny. That's what this is. It was your destiny to come to Sleepy Hollow."

Isabela twisted a stray string hanging from her shorts around her finger. "Destiny can be weird."

Becky hugged Isabela. "We'll be your family if that's all right."

"Yeah," Honey said. "Sisters. We'll be your sisters."

Isabela smiled, but just as it seemed like she was about to say something, Bart barked like mad at three squirrels racing around a tree trunk. He clambered to his feet and chased them.

"Hang on," Becky said. "Don't let him go."

"I won't," Isabela said. "But help me, please. He is soooooo strong."

All three Howlers held Bart's leash and pulled him away from the tree. The squirrels

scurried into the treetop and disappeared in the branches.

"Come on," Honey said. "Let's get him back."

"Good idea," Isabela said.

"Can you walk tomorrow?" Honey asked.

"No," Isabela said. "I am working at the shelter. The Barkathon, remember? You should come. Maybe someone will adopt Stormy, and you can kind of check them out."

167

"Great idea," Honey said. "We'll come after we take Bart for his first walk."

"Good," Isabela said. "It will be fun. They're gonna have hot dogs and popcorn."

"Yayyy," Becky said. "And we should wear our shirts. We might get some more business."

"Good idea," Honey said.

The Howlers hugged. Isabela swiped away a tear. "I like having sisters. I just wish—"

"Wish what?" Honey asked.

"It could be forever," Isabela said.

Of course, as Honey and Becky made their way back across the green they ran into Clarice again. This time she was walking a bulldog.

"Hey, losers," Clarice said. "I got two more clients. How many did you get?"

Honey didn't say anything right away. But Becky did.

"Aww, come on, Clarice. We don't care about your dumb bet. We like the dogs we have just fine."

"Just a loser's way of saying they're losing."

Honey shrugged. "Someday, Clarice Kligore, I predict you'll figure out that it's not necessary to be so mean." Then she turned and walked off with Becky.

"But seriously, Becky," Honey whispered. "We need more dogs."

A New Home for Stormy

The next morning, Honey awoke feeling excited. Not only was she going to walk the dogs but she was also going to the adoption event at the shelter. And not only that, but now that Stormy was out of isolation, she might even get a chance to play with her. It was going to be the best day ever!

Honey dressed, making sure to wear her new Howlers T-shirt. She looked in the mirror. "Here's to a great day." She spied Turtle in the mirror. He was hanging on her bedpost, looking a little limp.

"What's up, Turtle?" she asked into the mirror.

Nothing. All she had was the usual feeling she had when Turtle was around. All was well, and all would be well no matter what happened. Harry was always saying that having a friend like Rabbit—Harry's invisible sidekick—had consequences. Honey thought having a backpack like Turtle had some consequences also. Like having people look at you like you just slid off your rocker when you were talking to him and not caring what people thought. But Turtle also had a way of helping Honey feel like she had some great missions in life—not just now but in the future.

She grabbed Turtle and looked into his googly eyes. "Right now my mission is to help Isabela."

Tuttle didn't respond. But Honey knew Isabela was definitely an important part of her life right now.

She slung him over her back and headed down to breakfast.

Honey sat at the table. Her mom was home today making French toast, Honey's favorite breakfast.

"How come you're home?" Honey asked.

171

"Day off," Mary Moon said as she flipped a slice of French toast. "I'm working a double shift tomorrow."

Honey sipped orange juice. "After I walk Mrs. Tenure's corgis and Bart, the Saint Bernard, I'm going to the adoption event at the shelter."

Mary Moon placed a plate of the delectable breakfast in front of Honey. The slices were already covered with powdered sugar, but Honey also added gobs of goopy syrup.

"What kind of event?" Mary asked.

"Isabela said it's one of Mayor Kligore's things. It's called the Spooktacular Barkathon."

"Oh, yes, I saw a poster at the market. It's a good cause, I suppose."

Mary Moon did not always like Mayor Kligore's events, but Honey was pleased her mom thought this one sounded like a good thing. Helping stray animals is a nice thing.

172

∾

Honey and Becky had an easy time with Bart. He seemed a little sad or something.

"Maybe he misses Isabela," Becky said.

"Could be. He really does like her."

Manny, Moe, and Jack, on the other hand, were a little more rambunctious. For one thing, Moe bit the heads off three of Mr. Jay's chrysanthemums.

"No," Honey called when she saw the dog chewing yellow petals. "Spit that out." She knocked on Mr. Jay's door. He wasn't home, so she left a note.

"I hope he won't be too upset," Honey said.

"At least he only ate three of them." Before she finished speaking, Jack pulled his leash out of Becky's hand and went dashing after a tiny poodle. The chase didn't last long. The little poodle squeezed through her doggie door.

173

"Phew," Honey said. "Come on, let's get these guys home." She huffed and puffed a little from running so hard.

"Yes," Becky said. "I think we earned our fee this morning. It would have been easier with Isabela."

Honey opened the front yard gate at Mrs. Tenure's house. "Let's get right over to the Barkathon. I don't want Stormy to get adopted without me."

The Sleepy Hollow Animal Shelter was dressed to the nines—the K-9s that is. There were banners and flags on the outside. One read "Kligore Spooktacular Barkathon—Have a Howling Good Time." She did not like the fake dog skeletons with scary, red eyes on the grass, though. Neither did Becky.

But when they walked through the front door things definitely looked happier. And even funnier. A lot of the dogs were wearing Halloween costumes. They saw dogs dressed as Batman,

Wonder Woman, the Headless Horseman, and even one that was probably supposed to be Maximus Kligore.

"They look so cute," Becky said. "I like the one dressed up like a Smurf."

But then Honey laughed so hard she almost lost her breath. A wiener dog dressed as a hotdog was paraded past them by Terry, the reception lady.

"Oh my, will you look at that precious doggie," said an older woman standing near Becky. She pointed at the wiener dog. "I have to have her."

Honey nudged Becky. "I'll say one thing for Mayor Kligore. He sure knows how to get dogs adopted."

Honey made her way through the crowd— some of whom were sipping puppy punch and munching on dog-bone shaped cookies, at least Honey hoped they were people cookies. They were. Becky snagged one for each of them.

"Yum," Honey said. "These are terrific. Lemony."

"Do you see Isabela?" Becky asked.

"Not yet," Honey said looking around. Then she spied her standing in a corner speaking with Mrs. Stevens. Isabela was dressed in a veterinarian costume—which really wasn't much different than what she usually wore at the shelter. Except, this time, she had a stethoscope hanging from her neck.

176

"Hey, look," Honey said. "There she is."

"I wonder why she's here," Becky said.

"She works here," Honey said.

"No, I mean Mrs. Stevens."

Honey grabbed another cookie. "Maybe she wants another dog."

"Yikes, Bart barely fits in their house now as it is."

"Should we go over there?" Honey asked.

Becky seemed to be thinking a moment. "I don't know. They look pretty serious."

"Yeah, let's give them a few minutes. I want to find Stormy."

Honey took Becky's hand and weaved her way through the crowd.

"Looks like a lot of dogs will get adopted today," Becky said.

191

Honey stopped when she saw Stormy being led from the back by a woman she didn't recognize.

"There she is, but who is that person?"

"Probably a worker," Becky said.

Honey moved closer until she was directly in front of Stormy. She knelt. "There you are, Stormy. I was looking all over for you."

Stormy went nuts. She wagged her tail so hard she fell down on her rump. Honey hugged her around the neck, and Stormy kept licking Honey's face.

"She's really taken with you. I hope you aren't interested in adopting her?" the woman asked.

Honey continued to hug Stormy's neck. Stormy was enjoying every second of it. "Oh no, I was the one who found her and brought her here. I was hoping to see her get adopted today."

"Oh, that's good," the woman said with a sigh of relief. "Because there is someone interested in her."

"Oh, who?" Honey asked. "Isabela said I could check out the adopters."

The woman laughed lightly. "Well, it's a little unusual, but I assure you the people interested are terrific people."

"That's good." Honey squeezed Stormy one last time. "I know you were never really mine. And I'm glad you came into my life. But you're gonna have a great new home now."

Honey looked up at the shelter worker. "With kids?"

"With kids," the woman said.

"Hear that, girl?" Honey asked. "You're getting kids."

Stormy let out a loud bark. She wagged her tail. She jumped up on Honey, and Honey hugged her. "I'm glad I found you, and I'm even more glad you found a forever home."

Honey watched Stormy walk toward her new family. They were so happy. And the kids, a boy and a girl, squealed when Stormy licked their faces.

"You're like a hero," Becky said.

Honey shrugged. "Like I always say I just—"

"Go where you are needed," Becky said with a smile.

"Let's go find Isabela," Honey said.

By the time they got to Isabela, Mrs. Stevens was gone, and Isabela was sitting on a bench twisting another string around her finger.

Honey thought she was crying.

A STRANGER

oney and Becky walked closer to Isabela.

"Are you crying?" Honey asked. She put her hand on Isabela's shoulder.

Isabela looked up at her. "A little."

"Why?" Becky asked.

"Oh, it's just that Mrs. Stevens was here, and

she was really nice. We talked about all sorts of things—especially dogs and Bart."

"Why are you crying?" Honey asked.

"It was just nice to talk to someone like her. I thought she was real nice when we first met the other day. It makes me . . . it makes me miss my mom."

Honey sat on the bench and hugged Isabela. Becky joined in on the hug also.

182

After a few moments, Isabela said, "Did you hear? Some people were interested in Stormy. They said they'd be back after they went home and discussed it."

"Yes," Honey said. "Another worker was bringing Stormy out to them. At least I think it's them."

"Two kids, a boy and a girl. They're twins."

"Yes," Honey said. "That must have been them."

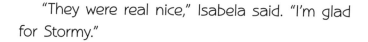

"They were real nice," Isabela said. "I'm glad for Stormy."

"They'll probably change her name," Becky said.

"Probably. Most new owners do." Isabela wiped her eyes on her smock.

Honey stood. "So, what now?"

"I guess you can mingle and stuff. The cookies are pretty good. I should go see if I can help anyone."

183

"Okay," Honey said. "And listen, you'll get a real family, too, one day. I just know it." Once again Turtle grew a little heavier.

Isabela smiled widely. "Thanks, I hope so."

Honey and Becky watched Isabela disappear behind the double doors.

"Why do you suppose Mrs. Stevens was here?" Becky asked.

"I don't know," Honey said. "It's like a mystery."

Honey was quiet at dinner that evening. She didn't feel very hungry, and she just kind of moved her peas around on her plate. It was hard not to think about Isabela. Even though Isabela was happy most of the time and Miss Mapleleaf was the sweetest old lady in Sleepy Hollow, Isabela still needed a real home.

"Are you feeling all right?" Honey's mom asked.

"Yes, I'm okay. Just thinking about my new friend Isabela."

"Oh, the girl from the shelter," Mary Moon said.

"Yep. She's so nice, and I just want her to not have to be a foster child anymore. It must be terrible to feel so . . . temporary. Did you know she's from Ecuador? She has no family in America. That's about as alone as a person can get."

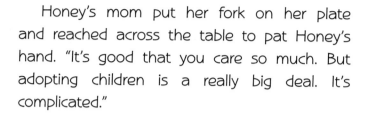

Honey's mom put her fork on her plate and reached across the table to pat Honey's hand. "It's good that you care so much. But adopting children is a really big deal. It's complicated."

"That's right," Honey's dad said. "And older kids are harder to place than babies."

Harry swallowed. "The Great Magician says no one will be left an orphan."

Honey tossed a pea at him. "How come you know so much about the Great Magician?"

"He's my best friend," Harry said.

Honey pushed her peas into her mashed potatoes. "Something else happened."

"What else?" Mary Moon asked.

"Well, today at the Barkathon, Mrs. Stevens was there. She was talking to Isabela. And Isabela said she was really nice, and they talked about a lot of things. But then Mrs. Stevens left, and it made Isabela sad."

"I see," Mary Moon said. "I'm sure it will be okay. Maybe you can call Isabela after supper and cheer her up."

Honey perked up. "That's a great idea. Can she come over and play?"

"Sure," Mary Moon said. "We can even drive over and pick her up."

Honey hurried through the rest of her supper. Then, since it was her turn to load the dishwasher, she hurried through that also. She even swept the floor, ran the trash out to the cans, and wiped down Harvest's booster seat.

"There," Honey said as she surveyed the kitchen. "Perfect. Now it's time to go get Isabela."

As Honey left the kitchen, her eyes caught a glimpse of the words stenciled around the Moon family dining room. Words that Honey

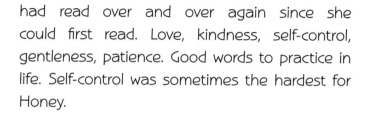

had read over and over again since she could first read. Love, kindness, self-control, gentleness, patience. Good words to practice in life. Self-control was sometimes the hardest for Honey.

Honey dashed upstairs, brushed her teeth, and grabbed Turtle. "Not sure if I'm gonna need you on this ride, but I like having you along."

"I'm ready to go, Mom," Honey called as she ran down the steps—only to be met by her father. "How many times must I tell you? Walk down the steps."

187

"Sorry, Dad," Honey said. "I'm just excited to go to Isabela's."

"I understand," her dad said. "But safety is important also."

Honey walked to the front door. "Come on, Mom, let's go."

"I'm coming, Honey," she called from the den. "Hold your horses."

Honey had her hand on the doorknob. She didn't really know why she was so excited to go to Isabela's. But she had an excited feeling inside like she was about to do something super important.

"Did you call or text her?" her mom asked as she grabbed her backpack from the hook near the front door.

"No, I think I'd rather surprise her. I'm sure it'll be okay."

Mary Moon shook her head. "Okey dokey, I hope you're correct."

"Of course, I am." Honey opened the door. "I'm mostly always correct."

"So she lives in the big house on the other side of town, right?" Mary Moon asked as she backed down the driveway.

"Right," Honey said. "Miss Mapleleaf's house."

"She's a sweet woman," Mary said. "I've met

her a couple of times. It's a good work she does taking in foster children."

"She's had other kids?" Honey asked. She was surprised. She hadn't thought about that before.

"From what I know, Miss Mapleleaf has cared for babies mostly."

"Oh, okay. That explains why I never met any other foster kids in town. I wonder why she took Isabela."

189

Mary Moon turned onto Broom Stick Drive. "Don't know."

"Destiny," Honey said. "I think it is destiny."

Mary Moon pulled up to the big, old house.

"Look," Honey said. "There are two cars in the driveway."

"So?" Mary said.

"Do you think they have company?"

"Don't know," Honey's mom said. "Why don't you text her?"

Honey grabbed her phone and texted Isabela. "Can you come out?"

A few seconds later her phone chimed. "In a few."

190

"Uhm," Honey said. "Let's just wait a couple minutes."

Honey kept her eye on the front door.

"Look," she said. "It's opening."

Honey pushed open the car and jumped out. But she stopped when she saw Isabela, Miss Mapleleaf, and another woman she had never seen before emerging from the house. The other woman was tall and skinny, and she carried a briefcase.

"Who is that?" Honey asked.

"I'm not certain," Mary Moon said. "But she could be Isabela's caseworker."

"Who?"

"Caseworker. She's the professional who follows Isabela's situation. Keeps tabs on her. Makes sure she's okay and stuff."

"Oh, that must be weird."

Honey watched as the woman with the

briefcase opened her car door.

"Can I go now?" Honey asked.

"Another minute," Mary Moon said.

But it was too late. Honey ran up the long walkway to the house as the woman backed down the driveway.

"Isabela," Honey called.

192

"Hi," Isabela said with a wave.

Honey panted a little when she reached the porch. "Sorry I didn't call. I was just hoping you could play."

Isabela looked at Miss Mapleleaf. Miss Mapleleaf nodded.

"How are you, Honey?" Miss Mapleleaf asked.

"I'm fine. How are you?"

Miss Mapleleaf smiled, and her already rosy

cheeks brightened. "I'm just fine also. So do you and Isabela have plans?"

"Not really," Honey said. "I just thought we could play. Maybe we can go to my house or the park." Honey looked at Isabela. But she seemed far away. Lost in her thoughts.

"Are you okay, Isabela?" Honey asked.

"Oh, sorry," she said shaking her head. "I think so. It's just that . . . that I got news."

193

"Good news?" Honey asked.

"Maybe."

"Now, now," Miss Mapleleaf said. "I think it might be best not to get ahead of yourself, Isabela. Let Mrs. Lewis do her job, and we'll see."

Now Honey was really confused. "Who is Mrs. Lewis?"

"My caseworker," Isabela said. "She just left. You saw her."

"Right," Honey said. "Is there something up with your case?"

"I'll say," Isabela said. "Something is definitely up."

CAN IT BE GOOD NEWS?

Honey and Isabela walked to Honey's car.

"Mom," Honey said. "Is it okay if Isabela and I just walk to the park?"

"Sure," Mary Moon said. "I'll pick you up here in about an hour and a half."

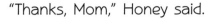

"Thanks, Mom," Honey said.

"Thanks," Isabela said.

Honey couldn't wait for her mom to drive off. She was dying to ask Isabela about what was going on with her case. And she didn't waste a single second once her mom drove down the street.

"So tell me," Honey said, "what's going on?"

"Nothing is definite, not yet. But Mrs. Lewis told me there is a couple who is looking for an older child to adopt." Isabela smiled, but she was also shaking.

Honey took her hand. "Wow! Seriously? Who?"

"I don't know," Isabela said. "Mrs. Lewis said the couple wants to come see me tomorrow. Right here. At this house."

Honey was lost for words. For the first time in her life, Honey did not know what to say. She just stood there looking at Isabela.

Isabela swiped away tears. Honey shrugged Turtle off her back. She hugged him to her chest and said, "This is going to sound weird, but would you like to hug Turtle? He has a way of making me feel better."

Isabela laughed and nodded through her tears as she pulled the Turtle backpack close. After a couple of moments, Isabela's tears dried. "You're right. I do feel better."

"Not everybody gets what it means to have a friend like Turtle. But I figured you might be one of them."

Isabela continued to hold the backpack while they walked toward the park.

"So you have noooooo idea in the whole world who these people are?"

"No," Isabela said. "I only know they are already here in Sleepy Hollow."

"Uhm," Honey said. "You don't say. Well, that is very interesting."

Isabela walked on. She was quiet the whole way to the park. "I love the swings."

"Me too," Honey said. "How high can you go? Do you like to get the bumps?"

"Yeah. Come on, I'll race you. First one to get the bumps wins."

"Okay," Honey said. She dropped Turtle on the ground. Honey pumped her legs harder and harder and harder, but Isabela won.

198

"Good job," Honey said. "Can you jump off?"

"I sure can." And *zoom!* In a second, Isabela was flying through the air and landed almost perfectly on the soft grass.

Honey followed, only her landing was not so graceful.

Isabela sat cross-legged. Honey did the same. She picked at the grass.

"I'm glad the people are from Sleepy

Hollow," Honey said.

"Me too." Isabela rolled the blade of grass around in her fingers. "I like it here. Even if it's a little strange with it always being Halloween. But that's kind of fun."

"Yeah, I guess. But mostly it just makes me feel creepy. I wish we could just be a normal town sometimes."

Honey tossed a small pebble.

199

"Normal." Isabela sighed. "I wish I could just be normal sometimes."

Honey felt a twinge in her stomach. She could not even begin to imagine what it would be like to not have her family—including Harry. "Maybe now you will."

"But what if I don't like them?"

Honey sighed. "You will. I have a feeling that they are going to be the perfect people. Just for you."

Isabela snagged Turtle and hugged him. "I hope so. I really hope so."

That night, Honey lay in her bed thinking about what getting adopted would feel like. As hard as she tried, she couldn't imagine. She, of course, had never experienced it. But then a car drove down the street, and the headlights shined through her window and lit Turtle's face.

"I guess I kind of adopted you," Honey said. "Or maybe you adopted me. Sometimes I think you came into this house just for me. Like you were made for me." Honey smiled and watched some shadows dance on the ceiling. Shadows that used to scare her but didn't anymore.

Honey closed her eyes, but she still couldn't fall asleep. She was terribly excited for Isabela and also worried. What if the people were mean? Nah, Honey shook her head. She was going to believe that whoever was visiting Isabela tomorrow would be the perfect people.

Morning came with a blast of cooler air. July was usually a hot month in Sleepy Hollow,

200

but every once in a while the wind blew chilly. Honey thought that was just another Sleepy Hollow phenomenon like how the air always smelled like autumn—burnt leaves and pumpkin spice.

Usually, on a morning like this, Honey would pull her blanket over her head and catch a few more Zs. But not this morning. She was too excited for Isabela. How she wished she could be a bug on the wall and listen in on the meeting. But no, she couldn't, and it really wasn't any of her business. She laughed. She laughed because she knew what Harry would say. "When has that ever stopped you?"

But no, this was too private. Too special. Honey would just have to wait until Isabela told her about it.

Honey not only had to walk the dogs, but she also had a list of chores to keep her busy. Her mom had already left for work, and Mrs. Wilcox was outside with Harvest when Honey went downstairs. Mary Moon always left a list on the refrigerator.

This morning's list was not too long, but before she read it completely, Honey noticed the picture of Anisha. "I'll be sending you a new desk soon," she said. "A few more walks and there should be enough to buy one. Of course, I have to pay Becky and Isabela."

The first task on her list was "swap out laundry."

Ugh. Of all the household chores, laundry was Honey's least favorite. But at least she only had to take the clothes in the dryer out and put them in a basket and put the clothes in the washer into the dryer. Easy peasy.

Honey practically tripped over Half Moon, who liked to laze about in the laundry room. He let out a little yelp but then settled back to his nap. "Sorry, boy," Honey said. "Guess I'm in a hurry."

She had just gotten the clothes, including Harry's boxer shorts, into the dryer when her phone chimed. It was a text from Becky. "Waiting 4 U."

"Oh geeze," Honey said. "I have to get Becky, and then we need to get to Mrs. Tenure's."

Honey finished her chores, grabbed her backpack, and scrammed out the door. Becky didn't know about Isabela's meeting today. By the time she got there she had decided that telling Becky about Isabela's meeting today was not tattling or passing on a rumor, and Isabela would not mind at all if Becky knew. Besides, the more people who knew the better they could support and encourage Isabela.

203

Honey saw Becky sitting on the porch. She was wearing her pink Sleepy Hollow Howlers T-shirt, blue shorts, and yellow sneakers.

"Hi," Honey called.

"About time," Becky said. "I was afraid you weren't coming."

"Ugh," Honey said. "I had to do some laundry."

Becky called to her mom. "I'm leaving."

"See you later, sweetie," Becky's mom called.

"So," Becky said. "The corgis first?"

"Yep."

"Wish Isabela was here. She makes it easier."

Honey stopped walking. She was practically jumping up and down. "Listen," she said, "I have something to tell you about Isabela."

"Ohhh, what is it?" Becky asked.

"Some people want to adopt her. They're from Sleepy Hollow, and they are meeting Isabela today."

Becky's eyes grew to the size of tea saucers. "No way. Really?"

Honey's head was nodding so hard it hurt. "I was there yesterday when her caseworker gave her the news. Well, not there, I was standing outside, and then Isabela told me the news. Right in front of Miss Mapleleaf and everything."

"This is great news," Becky said. "Do you know what time they're coming and what will happen? Does she just go with them?"

"I have no idea how it all works." Honey picked up her pace. "We better hurry. I'm sure Mrs. Tenure is wondering what happened."

"And you know how much she dislikes tardiness."

They laughed.

"Imagine that," Becky said. "Getting new parents when you are ten years old."

Honey walked a few paces. "Yeah. I can't imagine. But I can be happy for Isabela."

Mrs. Tenure was waiting on the porch.

"I'm sorry," Honey called. "I had to do the

laundry."

"Oh, that's fine," Mrs. Tenure said. "I knew you wouldn't let me down, Honey Moon."

"How are the boys?" Becky asked. "And how is your ankle?"

Mrs. Tenure leaned on her crutches as Honey opened the front door. "The boys are raring to go, and my ankle is on the mend. Doctor said three more weeks and the cast can come off."

Manny, Moe, and Jack were leaping off the ground. Moe licked Becky's face.

"They are happy to see us," Honey said.

"Where is Isabela?" Mrs. Tenure asked.

"Oh, she couldn't make it today." Honey attached the leash to Jack's collar and then Manny's. "She had some super important business today."

"I see," Mrs. Tenure said. "So you think you

two can handle this mob?"

"Absolutely," Honey said. "Isabela showed us some tricks and techniques."

"Good-o. Well, I'll see you in a little while."

Honey and Becky and the three dogs made their way down the street. Jack was pulling hard on the leash, and Honey tried to get him to walk the way Isabela showed her, but she wasn't having much success. Becky, on the other hand, had Moe, and he was walking quite nicely. Manny was doing a sort of half and half job.

The dogs stopped several times to sniff bushes and grass and fire hydrants and trees.

"Ugh," Becky said. "They sure do like the smell of things."

"Yeah, disgusting things," Honey said. "But, I guess when you're a dog, what's disgusting to us is like the smell of fresh baked apple pie to them."

Honey pulled Manny away from a rhododendron bush. "Manny, come on. Time to go home."

Manny let out a woof and that started Moe and Jack barking also.

"Ugh," Becky said. "Why are they barking?"

"I guess they're not ready to go home."

208

"Wow," Becky said as she pulled on Moe's leash. "Walking dogs is harder than I thought it would be."

"Yeah. We really need Isabela. I hope she can keep working with us."

The dogs settled into a nice walk with Honey and Becky. Honey even smiled and walked tall, feeling more confident than ever with them.

"So do you have any idea who these people meeting Isabela today are?" Becky asked.

"No. I just know they're from Sleepy Hollow."

They walked another block and arrived back at Mrs. Tenure's house.

"I don't think I'll ever get used to doing work for a teacher," Becky said. "It's weird."

Honey pulled the gate open, and all three of the dogs pulled away and dashed onto the porch.

"It is a little strange," Honey said. "But she really needs our help."

209

Mrs. Tenure was ready with their fee. "I hate to rush you today," she said. "But I have to make a doctor's appointment."

"That's okay, Mrs. Tenure," Honey said. "We understand. But I was hoping, since you're a teacher and all, that you will explain something to us."

Mrs. Tenure looked at the clock on the fireplace mantle. "Well, I have just a few minutes."

"How does a kid get adopted?" Honey asked.

Mrs. Tenure looked surprised. "Now, that's a tough question. There's a lot of paperwork and meetings, and they have to even go before a judge in court."

"Court?" Becky said. "Wow."

"Well, a judge needs to decide if the new family is fit to adopt a child and then he or she makes it legal."

210

"I can see why that's important." Honey rubbed and scratched Manny's ears. "Does it take long?"

Mrs. Tenure lifted herself to her feet using her crutches. "I need to get going, but to answer your question, I'm not sure. I think it can take a little time or maybe a long time. I think it depends on the situation."

Honey helped Mrs. Tenure to the door. "Well, I hope Isabela's adoption only takes a little time."

"Me too," Mrs. Tenure said. "Adoption is quite a change in a young girl's life. She'll have an adjustment period for sure."

Honey locked the front door and helped Mrs. Tenure into her car.

"It's good I broke my left ankle," Mrs. Tenure said. "I can still drive."

"That is good," Honey said. "If I could drive I would take you. I hope your appointment is good. See you tomorrow."

Honey and Becky watched Mrs. Tenure drive away.

"Wow," Honey said. "I never thought about how complicated getting adopted would be. Meetings. Court. A judge."

"I know," Becky said. "But I guess they need to be sure."

Honey headed down the walk. "We better get over to the Stevenses' house. Bart is probably out of his mind waiting on us."

212

BART ON THE LOOSE

When they arrived at the Stevenses' front gate, Honey noticed something strange. A car was parked in the driveway. And it wasn't Mrs. Stevens's car, but Honey thought she had seen it before.

"That's odd," Honey said. "Are they home? Why didn't they call?"

"Do you think she still needs us to walk

Bart?" Becky asked.

Honey pushed open the gate. She could hear Bart barking. "Come on," Honey said. "Let's find out."

Instead of getting the key from under the flowerpot, Honey knocked on the front door. She waited a few seconds and knocked again. Bart's barks grew louder. "I guess they're not home."

214

Honey retrieved the front door key and unlocked it. Bart practically jumped into her arms and knocked her back out onto the porch. "Slow down, big fella," Honey said. "We're here now."

Bart was so excited to see them you'd think he hadn't been walked in a month. He tried to jump on Becky also, but she pushed him away in a kind-hearted manner. "Someone needs to go out."

Honey snagged Bart's leash off the hook and attached it to his wide collar and said,

"Let's go."

Bart was trying his best to pull ahead of Honey. She tried to remember what Isabela taught her. But it was as though Bart was on a mission. He was heading a totally different direction than their usual route.

"Where's he going?" Becky asked.

"I don't know," Honey said. "But he is definitely determined to get somewhere."

215

"Maybe he has a girlfriend somewhere," Becky said.

Honey laughed. "I doubt that."

Bart continued to tug on the leash.

"He's heading for Folly Farm," Honey said.

"Oh no," Becky said. "I don't want to go there. That place always gives me the creeps."

"Me too," Honey said. "But let's see what he wants."

They had just reached the last street before Folly Farm when they saw Clarice walking down the street with a large, mean-looking German shepherd.

"Good morning, Clarice," Honey said.

The dog on Clarice's leash barked wildly. Bart snarled and barked back, although a snarl on a Saint Bernard is a little comical.

"This is Rex," Clarice said. "My fifth client. How many do you have?"

Honey pulled back on Bart's leash, and he settled back on his haunches with a look that said, "That Rex dog is just not worth it." Honey smiled and patted his head.

She thought about Clarice's question for a second and said, "Four." She was, of course, counting all three of Mrs. Tenure's corgis.

"I'm still winning," Clarice said. "And I have a meeting with Mrs. Snodgrass next to meet her dog, Simon—he's a mastiff."

Honey shrugged. At this point, she didn't really care anymore about winning the contest with Clarice. She was perfectly content with just the four dogs. But she didn't want Clarice to know that.

"Good luck," she said. "But we need to get walking."

Clarice sashayed past Honey and Becky with her nose in the air. "Come, Rex." Unfortunately, Rex chose just that moment to spy a squirrel, and he took off so hard and fast that Clarice fell into the grass face first. Honey suppressed her urge to laugh. Instead, Bart got to his feet and started to pull.

217

"Come on," Becky said. "I say we follow Bart."

"Maybe it's a treasure," Honey said.

Becky laughed. "I seriously doubt that."

Bart sallied forth. Determined. Single-minded. All Honey could do was follow until he finally stopped at the last street before the end of town. And there, sitting straight ahead on a small hill, was Miss Mapleleaf's house.

"Now, what in the world?" Honey said. "That's Mrs. Stevens's car."

Bart went a little crazy, wagging his big tail and barking.

"What a smart dog," Becky said. "He knew they were here."

"But why?" Honey asked. And then she snapped her fingers and said, "I know. I bet the Stevenses are the family interested in adopting Isabela."

Becky took such a deep breath she almost fell down. "Oh my gosh. You might be right. I mean why else would their car be here?"

"What should we do now?" Honey asked.

"I don't know, but I don't think we should just stand here. What if they come out? It's really none of our business."

Honey pulled on Bart's leash. "You're right. We better head back."

Honey tried to get Bart to run. She wanted to get as far away from Miss Mapleleaf's as possible. Bart reluctantly followed. "Come on, Bart," Honey said. "Let's get you home."

Honey and Becky both held onto Bart's leash. They made their way down the streets and to the Stevenses' house.

219

"What do you think," Honey asked. "Should we wait here until they come home?"

Becky shook her head. "I don't think that's very wise. I say we get Bart inside and scram. This is Isabela's business."

Honey nodded. "You're right."

After Bart was settled inside and the key was returned to its hiding place, Honey and Becky set off toward Honey's house.

Honey burst through the back door and into the kitchen where Mrs. Wilcox stood holding Harvest like a football, trying to wipe his face and hands.

"This child," Mrs. Wilcox said, "managed to get into every leftover mud puddle in the backyard."

Honey laughed. "He loves mud."

Harvest giggled while Honey and Becky helped Mrs. Wilcox get him cleaned up. Honey held his hands while Becky held his feet.

After Harvest was clean and shiny, Mrs. Wilcox took him to the living room to play with blocks, his absolute favorite toy. There is nothing like building towers and knocking them down. Honey and Becky played also.

"So how come you girls are sticking around here on such a nice day?"

Honey placed a red, square block on top of a yellow, cylindrical block. "We're waiting."

"Oh, yes," Becky said. She took a deep breath. "You see, we think our friend Isabela is getting adopted today."

Honey glared at Becky. "Don't say that. It might not be true."

Mrs. Wilcox sat on the floor. "Say what? How do you know all this? And who is Isabela?"

"She's the new girl who moved in with Miss Mapleleaf," Honey said. "She's a foster child, but we think the Stevenses are over there right now adopting her."

221

Mrs. Wilcox smiled and then looked startled as Harvest knocked over the tower. "Hold your horses. I don't think it happens just like that."

Honey sighed. "I know. Mrs. Tenure told us it takes courts and papers and lots of time, but we definitely think they are getting things started."

"So you like this Isabela?" Mrs. Wilcox asked.

"We sure do, and Mrs. Tenure said she's already registered for our class."

Mrs. Wilcox opened her mouth, but before she could get a word out, Honey's phone chimed. She slipped it out of her pocket. "It's Isabela."

"What does she say?" Becky asked. "Is she adopted?"

222

"She just says to meet her at the park. Now."

"Let's go," Becky said.

The girls scrambled to their feet. Honey grabbed Turtle and slung him over her back. "You're coming with me."

"Hold on, girls," Mrs. Wilcox said. "It might not be good news."

Honey swallowed and looked at Becky. She felt Turtle hug her back. Her heart sank into her sneakers. "She's right, Becky. Maybe we shouldn't act too excited until she tells us."

"Right," Becky said. "And besides, she doesn't know that we know."

Honey let out a chuckle. "You're right." She grabbed Becky's hand. "But I'm still really excited."

224

Isabela's News

"There she is," Honey said. "Over there." She pointed toward the Headless Horseman statue. It was pretty much the meeting place for everyone in Sleepy Hollow—the kids anyway. Honey waved.

Honey had a hard time *not* saying what was on her mind. She didn't want to let Isabela know that she had any inkling of the meeting. She remembered the words in the

dining room. Self-control.

"How are you?" Honey asked. "We missed you on the walks today."

"And the dogs missed you too, especially Bart," Becky said.

Isabela was looking at her shoes. Honey thought that wasn't a good sign. "Are you okay?" she asked.

226

Isabela looked up. She leaned against the statue's foundation. "I'm . . . I'm not sure."

"Are you sick?" Becky asked.

Isabela shook her head. "No, maybe just a little heart sick."

Honey could hardly contain herself. She wanted to blurt out that she knew the Stevenses visited her today. And she was just about to say something when Isabela said, "I might be getting adopted."

Now, when someone tells you she might be getting adopted, it's not exactly like she just told you she got a new bike. So Honey and Becky just stood there as still as old horseface.

Isabela nudged Honey. "Aren't you gonna say something?"

"I don't know what to say." Honey nudged her back.

Isabela started walking. "Let's go sit on the bench, and I'll tell you the whole thing. This horse dude gives me the creeps."

"Yeah, well, he's supposed to," Becky said.

A million ideas spun through Honey's mind as they walked across the park. Was this good news or bad news? Isabela did not seem the least bit excited, but maybe that's what it's like when you almost get adopted. Maybe she doesn't like the Stevenses. Honey had never met Mr. Stevens, so she had no way of knowing if he was nice or strict or tall or what

he even did all day.

Isabela sat on the bench. Honey sat with her, followed by Becky.

"It's the Stevenses," Isabela said. "They are thinking about adopting me. Turns out they can't have kids of their own. They wanted to adopt a baby—everybody wants a baby. But when Mrs. Stevens met me she said she got all swoony—that's what she called it. She said she couldn't stop thinking about me."

"Wowzers," Becky said. "That means you can stay in Sleepy Hollow and go to school with us and we can all still be friends and—"

"And," Honey said, "you can still be a Howler."

Isabela smiled. "I know. But I have to stay with Miss Mapleleaf for a while longer."

Now it was Honey's turn to feel a little sad. But she didn't want Isabela to know. She leaned down and picked up a small stick, which she tossed across the field. "Well, I for one think it's a great idea, and you are going to love living here."

Isabela shrugged. "It's not definite yet. We still have to spend time together and do all the court stuff—all the legal stuff."

"It will go fast," Honey said. "And you can be sure we'll be right here beside you the whole time. We will always be sisters even if we have the whole country between us."

Isabela's shoulders lifted clear to her ears as she took a deep breath. "The funny thing is, this whole thing has made me miss my real mom and dad again—more than ever. Mrs. Lewis said that was to be expected. But still . . ."

Honey had no words. But she didn't need any because Clarice came prancing by with a teeny, tiny, black poodle on the end of a skinny leash.

"Now that's more your size," Honey said.

Clarice stopped walking. "She might be small, but she's got quite a bark. And besides, I get the same fee for a large dog as a small dog."

Isabela raised her hand. "Hey, Clarice."

Clarice jutted her chin toward Isabela. "How's it going, foster kid?"

Honey got to her feet quickly. "Hey, don't call her that."

"Yeah," Becky said.

"It's all right," Isabela said. "It doesn't bother me anymore. And I guess I'd rather live with Miss Mapleleaf than in the spooky, old mansion any day."

The little dog pulled the leash and barked. Clarice was correct. Her bark was loud.

"See you around," Clarice said.

Honey, Becky, and Isabela stayed at the park for a little while longer. Isabela told them a little more about how the whole adoption thing would work. At first, Honey thought it sounded almost impossible, but when Isabela said, "And you know what? I really like Rob and Grace. And, of course, Bart," Honey knew it was going to happen.

A few weeks later, another big thunderstorm blew into Sleepy Hollow. The last thing Honey wanted to do was walk seven wet dogs, but she had made a commitment. And as long as the rain wasn't too cold, walking wasn't too bad. And now that they had seven clients, she and Becky and Isabela were busier than ever.

Isabela couldn't make it for some reason, so Honey and Becky were left to walk all the dogs. And it was going pretty well until their new client, a mutt named Fred, decided that rolling around in a fresh mud puddle was great fun. By the time Honey and Becky got him walking again, they were all covered with mud.

"We better get changed," Becky said.

Honey looked at her phone. "We can't. We're

late for Bart now as it is. And besides, we're just gonna get even wetter and maybe even muddier."

"I guess so," Becky said.

Honey and Becky headed over to the Stevenses' house to walk Bart. When they arrived, they saw Isabela sitting on the porch with Mrs. Stevens and Bart, who was sitting at Isabela's side.

232

Honey waved, and when Isabela saw her, she went tearing down the walkway. She was laughing. "You guys look like monsters from the mud lagoon."

"We feel like monsters from the mud lagoon," Honey said.

"Listen to this," Isabela said. "You'll never guess."

Honey and Becky looked at each other. They could probably guess, but they knew it would be better if Isabela told them.

"What," Honey said. "We can't guess."

Isabela took a breath. "We decided. Rob and Grace and Bart and me. We are definitely going to be a family."

Honey felt tears well up. Becky was already sobbing like a baby. Honey looked up at Mrs. Stevens who was standing with Bart. She was pretty sure Mrs. Stevens was also crying. Even Bart had a look of joy.

233

Honey threw her arms around Isabela. "I am so happy for you."

"Me too," Isabela said. "I can hardly believe it."

"Hey, girls," Mrs. Stevens called. "Are you still gonna walk Bart? He's champing at the bit."

"We sure are," Honey called.

"Wait for me," Isabela said. But then she stopped and looked at Mrs. Stevens. "Is it okay?"

Mrs. Stevens nodded. "Of course. Go. Have fun."

Isabela ran up the walkway and into the house. A few minutes later she came out wearing a pink Sleepy Hollow Howlers T-shirt.

The howlers headed down the street with Bart leading the way. They rounded the corner onto Broom Stick Drive and ran smack dab into Clarice. She was struggling with four dogs.

"Stop it," Clarice yelled at Rex, the German shepherd. "Stop smelling things and come!"

Honey, Becky, and Isabela laughed.

Clarice ignored them at first. But then, all of a sudden, Rex and Simon pulled so hard on the leash that Clarice went flying head first into a mud puddle. Honey had to put her hand over her mouth to keep from laughing.

"Have a nice trip, Clarice?" Becky asked.

Clarice was now sitting in the mud. The

dogs had run off barking. Honey thought Clarice looked like she wanted to cry.

"We'll help you get the dogs back," Honey said. She reached her hand down to help Clarice up when she lost her footing and went into the puddle with a *smack!* Becky tried to help Honey up, but she too went *smack!* into the puddle.

Only Isabela was left standing. "Sorry, girls," she said, "but there is no way—"

Too late. Honey and Becky grabbed her hands and with a *smack!* Isabela landed in the puddle. Bart, on the other hand, didn't need any help getting into the mud. Even Turtle landed

in the gooey abyss. At least he landed on his back. His googly eyes were still above the mud.

They laughed and laughed. Even Clarice finally laughed. Then Clarice said something Honey never thought she would hear her say. "What is it with you and that turtle?"

Honey smiled. "I will tell you all about it someday."

"Better grab him," Becky said. "I think he's sinking."

Honey snagged the backpack and tossed it to higher ground, but when she did, mud sprayed everywhere making everyone laugh again. There was just something about getting muddy that felt so good and so fun.

"You know something, Clarice," Honey said, "I think this is the first time I ever heard you laugh."

Clarice didn't say anything for a moment. "I'm . . . I'm not laughing."

"Yes, you are," Becky said. "And you know what that means?"

"What?" Clarice said.

"That we officially adopt you to be our friend."

"Sometimes friend," Honey said. "When you're nice or when you fall head first into a mud puddle."

Clarice shook her head, sending mud flying everywhere. "I still won the contest, and you owe me a pizza."

"Then you'll need a little sauce," Isabela said, and she picked up a handful of mud and plopped it onto Clarice's head. "Welcome to the friends forever club."

ONE MONTH LATER

Honey dashed home after a hard day walking dogs. Boy, was she beat. But when she opened the kitchen door her mom was standing there holding an envelope.

At first, Honey thought she was in trouble. "What's that?" she asked.

"A letter. From Anisha."

Honey's spirits lifted. "Really? What does she say? Can I read it?"

"Sure."

Honey took the letter and read:

238

Dear Moon Family,

I am writing this to you while I sit at my new homework desk. It is made of wood and has two drawers. One I can lock so my brother can't sneak my candy when I get it. Thank you for sending me this desk.

Love,
Anisha

Honey swiped some tears from her eyes. "You know, Mom, I just have to say this has been a most successful summer."

"It sure has, Honey Moon. It sure has. Now, how about spreading some of that success to the laundry room?"

"Folding and putting away?"

Mary Moon nodded.

"I'm on it," Honey said. "I always go where I am needed."

239

240

SOFI'S LETTER

Hey there!

Wow! That was fun. I hope you enjoyed reading about Honey Moon's latest pet project. Did you know there are about seventy million stray animals in the United States? That's a lot of dogs and cats. I am so glad Honey Moon got to help Stormy. But who would ever think that finding a stray dog could lead to something so amazing for Isabela? And who would ever think that living in such a spooky town could bring good things?

241

Honey Moon knows. She is brave enough to get involved. That takes courage. And you know what else takes courage? Being yourself. It is brave to believe that you are a unique, precious young lady no matter what your feelings might be saying. The best part of being unique is not having to be perfect. It's okay to live in imperfection as long as you work on loving your reflection.

Sometimes a girl can feel as lost and alone as Stormy. So, that's why I started Bravehoneys. com. This is a safe place where you can go and read about other girls like you, like Honey, who are also learning to be brave in a sometimes scary world.

242

In my own life, I have discovered that it's easier to be brave with friends around to help. I am here to help, to remind you that you are not alone, that together we can lift each other up. Let's build a friendship based on this— fearless girls reaching their dreams. So, come visit me at Bravehoneys.com and together we'll BE BRAVE! Don't allow anything to dim your light.

Sparkle away!

Love,

Sofi ♥

MARK ANDREW POE

Honey Moon creator Mark Andrew Poe never thought about creating a town where kids battled right and wrong. His dream was to love and care for animals, specifically his friends in the rabbit community.

243

Along the way, Mark became successful in all sorts of interesting careers. He entered the print and publishing world as a young man, and his company did really, really well. Mark also became a popular and nationally sought-after health care advocate for the care and well-being of rabbits.

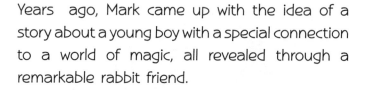

Years ago, Mark came up with the idea of a story about a young boy with a special connection to a world of magic, all revealed through a remarkable rabbit friend.

Mark worked on his idea for several years before building a collaborative creative team to help him bring his idea to life.

Harry Moon was born. The team was thrilled when Mark introduced Harry's enchanting sister, Honey Moon. Boy, did she pack an unexpected punch!

In 2014, Mark began a multi-book project to launch *Harry Moon* and *Honey Moon* into the youth marketplace. Harry and Honey are kids who understand the difference between right and wrong. Kids who tangle with magic and forces unseen in a town where "every day is Halloween night." Today, Mark and the creative team continue to work on the many stories of Harry and Honey and the characters of Sleepy Hollow. He lives in suburban Chicago with his wife and his twenty-five rabbits.

Honey Moon's
DNA

Builds friendships that matter
Goes where she is needed
Helps fellow classmates
Speaks her mind
Honors her body
Does not categorize others
Loves to have a blast
Seeks wisdom from adults
Desires to be brave
Sparkles away
And, of course, loves her mom

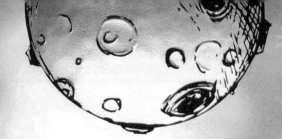

COMING SOON!
MORE MAGICAL ADVENTURES

POSTER INSIDE!

HONEY MOON

SCARY LITTLE CHRISTMAS

SOFI BENITEZ

Harry Moon's
DNA

Helps his fellow schoolmates
Makes friends with those who had once been his enemies
Respects nature
Honors his body
Does not categorize people too quickly
Seeks wisdom from adults
Guides the young
Controls his passions
Is curious
Understands that life will have trouble and accepts it
And, of course, loves his mom!

FOR MORE BOOKS
& RESOURCES GO TO
HARRYMOON.COM